C.A. VARIAN

GODDESS

OF

DEATH

SUPERNATURAL SAVIORS' SERIES
BOOK TWO

To CJ,
There's a monster
inside all of us.

CaV

CONTENTS

About the Author

TRIGGER WARNING

There are mature themes throughout this book, and it is not intended for readers under 17 years of age.

The following themes are explored in Goddess of Death: Graphic (consensual) sexual content, captivity, slavery, abduction, torture, vulgar language, and murder.

ORORIS

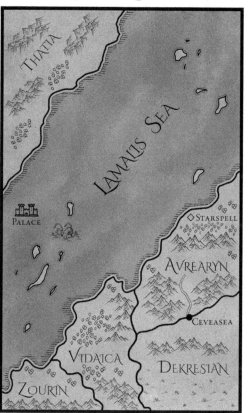

PROLOGUE

In the novel Song of Death, Ocevia Kallallis is a side character, a woman who was cursed as a child to live her life as a killer mermaid, but there is so much more to her story. In Song of Death, she is the best friend of the main character, Azure. Now it's time to read Ocevia's story from the beginning.

CHAPTER 1

THE BARGAIN

"**A**s long as you wear this, the beast inside you will remain hidden."

Eleven-year-old Ocevia Kallallis held the seashell necklace in her trembling fingers as tears slipped down her cheek, the weight of it so much more than her tiny mind could carry. The Sea Goddess, Miris, stood before her, having only just made a bargain with her family, a bargain that would take her away from them. *Forever.* It wasn't Ocevia's fault. She knew that. Even so, her true nature, the creature she became when she was angry or scared, had become too much for her parents. Unable to handle the destruction Ocevia created, her parents had summoned the Sea Goddess, agreeing to things she wasn't old enough to understand, no matter how many times they repeated the conditions to her.

"Will I be able to see my mommy again? My daddy?" Her small voice cracked, emotions flooding her like a wave about to crest. Although she asked the question, she already knew the answer. The Sea Goddess' enslaved mermaids were forbidden from visiting the human lands. Once she left her kingdom of Thatia, she would never be able to return. She would never see her family again. The dying hope threatened to shatter her innocence, extinguishing her fire for life.

With her silver mermaid tail transformed into legs, the Sea Goddess towered above the little girl, looking down at her with swirling quicksilver eyes. Even when Miris tried to look kind, she was still intimidating, nothing like Ocevia's mother, who was all softness.

Miris touched the seashell on Ocevia's necklace, letting the object slide through her long, elegant fingers. "My mermaids are not allowed to visit the human lands, little fish. Unless your family dares a trip into the sea, you will not be able to see them again, but do not cry. We will be your family."

Ocevia didn't want a new family. She wanted her mommy, daddy, and baby sister, but she knew better than to argue with the Sea Goddess. Her rules were not to be broken, and the last thing Ocevia wanted was more punishment.

Nodding and wiping the tears from her cheek, the little girl turned toward the Lamalis Sea, the place that would be her home for the rest of her life. She shivered looking at the vastness of the sea darkened by an incoming storm.

Even with Miris beside her, she'd never felt so alone. She'd already left her home high in the mountains with Miris that morning, and they'd traveled for hours back to where the water met the land. There were no more goodbyes to give. Her family was gone.

Everything in her wanted to break down, to fall to her knees and never leave the beach, but she knew what she'd done. The innocent lives lost because she was a monster, even if she'd never meant to hurt anyone. She understood why her parents had made the bargain, but it was for life and she was only a child. All she wanted was to go home.

There would be no way for her to go home, however. Living as one of Miris' mermaids required her to take lives—fifty thousand of them over her lifetime—but it was nothing compared to the horror she could cause in her true form. Not only would she kill droves, but she would be hunted to the ends of her world. She had to keep the monster hidden, and the only way she could do that was with Miris' magic. The tradeoff was so much bigger than she could comprehend at her age, but she'd been given no choice. The adults had determined her sentence and she was too young to fight it.

A numbing coolness washed over her. She forced away the burning behind her eyes, knowing weeping was useless. All she could do was be strong and focus on her new role in life, even if she didn't want to.

"When do we leave?"

Standing beside her in the sand, Miris pulled a dagger from a sheath on her thigh and reached for Ocevia's hand. Before the child knew what was happening, pain erupted like fire as the Sea Goddess sliced across her palm, the crimson blood soaking into the golden sand. Only a moment later, the young girl fell to her knees, her legs collapsing beneath her, and when she looked down, they were gone, replaced by an iridescent turquoise tail.

CHAPTER 2

10 YEARS LATER

"**H**old still. I'm almost done." Ocevia blew on her best friend's back as she screwed the lid back on the ointment tin. The wounds from her lashing were deep, still oozing blood in some places. "They should scab over soon. If you would stop defying her, she would stop having you whipped."

Ocevia knew she was right, but Azure couldn't seem to stay out of trouble. The wounds on her friend's back made Ocevia relieved she'd never been on the receiving end of the whip, and she intended to keep it that way. Miris' temper was reason enough to follow her rules.

Azure blew out a pained breath. "Even if I stayed out of trouble, she would still find a reason to punish me."

"You're probably right." Leaning forward, Ocevia rinsed her hands in the salty water. Waves crashed violently against their small cove, making it a dangerous place to rest, at least for humans. Mermaids like them, however, spent many daylight hours on the small, rocky islands that dotted the Lamalis Sea. "Are you going to be ready to go back out tonight?"

Azure glanced at the dozens of markings carved into the cave wall behind them before turning her eyes back to Ocevia. Although she pretended not to notice, Ocevia knew exactly what her friend was thinking. When the Sea Goddess had brought Azure's younger sister back to life after she drowned, Azure had been given no choice but to agree to repay five thousand souls, but so far, she had only managed to carve one hundred forty-three marks on the cave wall. She had a long way to go before being given her freedom to return to the human lands and to her sister.

Faded memories of Ocevia's own family fluttered into her mind, but she pushed them back, touching the shell necklace lying against her chest as a reminder. They'd thrown her away like garbage, but it had been a long time since then, too long to still grieve for them. She doubted they were grieving for her, even if she hoped they still did.

"I don't think I have a choice. My back can't take any more lashings just yet," Azure said.

Brushing her long hair away from her face, Ocevia pursed her lips, taking in her friend's tarnished skin, angry scars crossing her back where smooth porcelain skin had once been. The two were the same age, but Azure had spent the first eighteen years of her life as a human. After spending so long as a human, becoming one of Miris' enslaved mermaids had been a challenge for Azure. She rebelled more than the other mermaids did, earning beatings often. Secretly, Ocevia wished her friend would just conform because she worried about her, but she couldn't bring herself to tell Azure how to live her life.

Azure turned to look at her, her turquoise eyes, like those of all mermaids, resembling the water of the sea. She was truly beautiful, with thick, violet-tinged black hair that fell to the middle of her back, bringing out her bright eyes and sultry lashes. Ocevia glanced down at her own hair, blond like the sun and a tiny bit wavy, running her petite fingers through the tangles.

Their angelic voices, like their appearances, served a purpose. It was impossible for human men to ignore the song of a mermaid. As soon as they heard the song and saw the stunning creatures of the sea, sailors lost control of their ships and their willpower. Trying to claim the mermaid for themselves, they drowned in the dark waters. With each life the sea took, the mermaid was able to pay back her debt to Miris, bringing them one step closer to once again becoming human. For some, for Ocevia, freedom would never come, but the decision not to feed souls to the sea was not one any of the mermaids could make. It would be considered defiance and would be punished brutally.

"You really don't. You'll never be free if you keep putting more marks on your back than on that wall." Ocevia gestured to the back of the cave as she held her friend's stare, the injured mermaid sitting up with a grunt. She winced as the wounds on her back stretched with the movement. "Yeah... that's going to hurt you for a while."

Although Ocevia understood why her friend disobeyed Miris, and although she didn't want to be a killer either, it was the curse they'd been given. They didn't have the freedom or power to make those decisions for themselves.

"I'm aware. I'm the one who always takes the whip, after all. Have *you* ever even been punished by Miris?"

Looking out over the horizon, Ocevia inhaled, thinking of her time as a mermaid. She didn't remember everything, especially not from her life before, but she knew why she was cursed into this form, and it wasn't in exchange for a life debt. Her bargain was made because her true form was even more dangerous, more unpredictable, than a mermaid. Her own family had been afraid of her. She didn't recall much about them, but she did remember that.

The smell of briny water filled the moist cave as the sound of waves crashing against the jagged rocks echoed throughout the space. She remained silent for a long time before answering Azure's question, not because she didn't know the answer, but more because she realized how helpless she had become in her own life. Her power had been taken on that stormy day ten years prior and she'd never gotten it back. "I have not."

For only a moment, Ocevia came close to opening up to her friend and telling her about how she'd gotten there, about how she'd become enslaved, but she couldn't. She didn't want Azure to be afraid of her like her only family had been. So, instead of letting Azure in, Ocevia neutralized her expression, the cloudy look in her eyes clearing as she continued. "It's a stormy one today. Bad for the sailors, good for us."

Sighing, Azure pulled her breast band back on. Mermaids were meant to allure their victims, so there was no room for modesty. Most wore no coverings at all. "I don't consider it good for me either. I never wanted to be a killer."

Their stares locked, but Azure's face softened, silver lining her brilliant turquoise eyes. Ocevia knew how her friend felt about killing, but there was no way to get out of the bargain. Miris was dangerous, and she didn't allow disobedience. "The sea takes lives. We're just bystanders."

Azure let out an incredulous huff as she tucked her onyx hair behind her ear, and Ocevia knew the conversation wasn't over. She also knew she hadn't meant the words she'd spoken. She'd only said them in an attempt to make her friend feel better and had clearly failed.

Instead of trying to defend her statement, Ocevia turned and walked toward the cave they used for shelter during the daytime. Azure crawled to her feet, following her.

Although mermaids could shift into human forms and use their legs, they were not allowed to enter any human settlements. Therefore, most spent their time in caves and on uninhabited islands. Some also chose to rest in underwater caverns or the Sea Goddess' undersea palace. However, Ocevia had preferred to remain away from Miris even before she'd met Azure three years prior. Azure seemed to feel the same

"That's just wishful thinking, and you know it," Azure said, cynicism lacing her tone. "Most of those ships would make it safely across if it were not for us. She has turned us into monsters. The sea is the weapon, but we are the ones who wield it to claim the victims."

Ocevia knew her friend was right. Killing ate away at her conscience as well, no matter how much she tried to pretend she wasn't a monster. Tears stung her eyes, and she sniffed as she turned away, wiping her cheek and hoping Azure couldn't sense her weakness. Even though they were friends—best friends—Ocevia had never been able to let anyone all the way in. No one knew her secret except Miris, and she intended to keep it that way.

"We don't have a choice, Azure. You try to deny our fate, but all it does is get you beaten. It's not getting you any closer to seeing your sister again. Surely you must know this."

At least Azure would have a chance to see her family again. Ocevia almost said it, but she bit her tongue. Her curse wasn't her friend's fault, and Ocevia's family had all but thrown her at the Sea Goddess. It wasn't Azure's fault that Ocevia owed fifty thousand souls to Miris, a number set so high to make sure she never earned her freedom.

Azure placed her hand on Ocevia's elbow, her voice softening. "I know. Look, I'm sorry. I just hate this."

Ocevia hated it too, but all they had was each other. She wrapped Azure in her arms and cried silent tears on her friend's shoulder, needing physical contact. "I do too. We are all in this together. None of us want to live like this."

Trying to lighten the mood, Azure snorted. "I can think of a few who might. The *merbitches*."

Two of Miris' mermaids, Oona and Lucia, had forsaken their human lives, choosing to remain in their cursed form to be Miris' right hands. They were evil to their very cores and enjoyed bullying the other mermaids. They enjoyed killing, reveled in it.

Stifling a laugh, Ocevia nodded against Azure's shoulder, her mood only slightly improving. "Come on. Let's get something to eat."

CHAPTER 3

A PAINFUL PAST

Opening the crates lining the back of their cave, Azure grabbed some pieces of fish, a meal they were both tired of eating. Still, Ocevia chose to be grateful for the meal, for as meager and unappetizing as it was, it was still something. Fish made up most of their meals, either dried or fresh, but they were equally unappetizing.

Nevertheless, Ocevia nibbled on the paper-thin strips of meat while holding her nose, swallowing it down with a grimace

"I could really go for something other than dried fish right now."

A snicker escaped Azure's lips. "Me too. I don't remember my mother's cooking, but my father made a tasty stuffed goose. I could go for either at this moment."

"That sounds delicious. I don't actually remember my mother's cooking either, but I can imagine she was great at it." A deep melancholy settled inside Ocevia's chest, threatening to overshadow anything bright in her heart. She didn't remember her family enough to miss them, which stung just as much. Thoughts of them always brought up a chaotic mixture of emotion she didn't know how to navigate. "When I gain my freedom, you must take me to meet your family."

The look on her friend's face made Ocevia regret bringing up their families at all. "All that's left is my little sister. I hope she found a home with someone who cares for her. With only one hundred and forty-three souls after three years, my sister will be grown and married by the time I'm free." Azure shrugged, her eyes going distant. "With my luck, she will have moved away, and I'll never be able to find her."

"I'm sorry, Azure. I didn't mean to bring that up. I didn't realize about your parents."

Warmth filled Ocevia's insides as Azure squeezed her hand. It had been years since she last had a family, and Azure was the closest thing she had to a sister she could remember. She couldn't help but feel a spark of hope for the future; for the first time in a long time, she knew she was not alone. "No. It's okay. It's my fault for never telling you about them. I've moved past that loss."

"I understand. It's hard to bring up things that cause us pain, especially when we are supposed to be hardened out

here." Perhaps that was why Ocevia executed the indis-
criminate killing she was commanded to do. After doing it
for so long, she had built unbreakable stone walls around
her heart. She had completely insulated herself from emo-
tional pain, making it easier for her to do whatever was
asked of her without hesitation or regret. There were
times when her misdeeds haunted her at night without
her permission, but she always pushed the thoughts away
quickly. It did no good for her to dwell on the past.

There was an uncomfortable shift in Ocevia's posture
as Azure met her eyes, more due to her vulnerability than
due to the cold stone beneath her.

"And what about your family? Will I ever be able to meet
them?"

In terms of her past, Ocevia avoided discussing it as
much as she could. The reasons why she was enslaved to
Miris, and the topic of her family, were off limits, even to
Azure. Sighing, she fidgeted with the shell necklace that
concealed her true form. It never left her neck, a silent
weight that reminded her of where she'd come from and
what she truly was. "Maybe someday."

In truth, she lied. There would never be another time
for her to see her family, nor would Azure ever have the
opportunity to meet them. There was nothing she could
do but hope that her friend didn't have to suffer through
the same thing. Azure's sister, Daneliya, was everything
to her, and her friend's desire to return to her sister was
the most important thing in the world to her. Even if she
would never see her own family again, Ocevia vowed to
herself that she would help Azure pay back her life debt,

even if she had to sacrifice the souls she'd collected to do so. She would help Azure return to her little sister.

CHAPTER 4

SIREN SONG

Azure and Ocevia stepped outside their cave as a tempest threatened to rage around them. Severe storms always had the potential to help them sink ships, allowing them to claim souls, but they also limited the number of ships that could cross the sea. Storming or not, they were given no choice but to hunt at night. Azure's back was proof of that. Taking souls weighed on Ocevia's conscience, and it never got easier, but she knew it was harder on Azure. Unlike Azure, who'd only been cursed by Miris three years prior, Ocevia had been doing the Sea Goddess' bidding for most of her life. She didn't have another life of experiences to fall back on.

"Usual spot?" Ocevia asked as she dropped to sit on the edge of the rock, her human legs turning into an iridescent turquoise tail.

They usually waited for ships near the southern shipping channel, closest to Ocevia's family's home in Thatia, where she'd lived before she was taken away. Nightfall was a busy time for mermaids looking for victims, so finding a place not already claimed was difficult. Lingering near Thatia always sent the sting of longing through Ocevia's chest, but she never could bring herself to find a new location. Since she had been forbidden from returning to the human lands for any reason, she had no idea whether her family still lived there or anywhere at all. The question didn't hurt as much as it had when she was younger, but it still stung. It always would.

Even though ships could navigate through many parts of the sea, they preferred to stay near the same stretches of water, since those were deeper than areas near the coast. Most of the ships in the channel belonged to merchants who transported goods from the mainland of Thatia to the other kingdoms that were accessible by water: Avrearyn, Zourin, and Azure's own homeland of Vidaica. On the other hand, there was also a threat of pirates who attempted to do harm on those seas, robbing merchant ships and wreaking havoc. Since pirates were deemed as dangerous nuisances, the mermaids tended to focus their attention on sinking the those ships first, but merchants were also regarded as fair game. Ultimately, souls were souls, and Miris didn't turn any away.

"Our usual spot works for me."

Changing into her mermaid form, Azure sat down beside Ocevia on the rocks. The two of them remained there for a moment, watching the darkened sky as thunderclouds rolled in before sliding into the water and disappearing under the surface. As they swam through the storm, the wind was so strong that it forced them to dive deeper. Lightning and heavy winds made swimming at the surface almost impossible.

After an hour of traveling, they reached their usual hunting grounds, lifted their heads above the surface and began scanning the horizon, looking for any signs of danger. The boats were nowhere to be seen, but that didn't mean one wouldn't pass through eventually. In the distance, a brilliant flash of lightning crisscrossed the darkened sky. The crackle drove Azure back below the surface while Ocevia remained above it.

"Anyone out on the water tonight is a fool," Azure said as her head resurfaced, her long onyx hair billowing around her like silk.

Staying above the surface, Ocevia treaded water while watching the sky. The rain didn't bother her as much as it bothered her friend, but she understood. "I admit that tonight doesn't seem like it will be very fruitful. The storm is too bad. Let's hang around for a bit, though. A ship could show up."

There was a moment of silence between them as they scanned the horizon, each absorbed in their own thoughts. A sinking feeling swept through Ocevia's stomach and she stiffened against the lapping waves. Ahead of her, the merbitches, Oona and Lucia, broke the water's surface. Just seeing them sent her hurt into a violent tumble.

"This is our spot," Azure hissed, her words filled with so much more venom than Ocevia felt capable of producing. "You need to find another location."

Oona spat, her cruel smile widening as Lucia circled around them like a feral animal. "You and your weak little friend do not own this water. We hunt where we choose. Go ahead. Try to take souls from us. It won't end well for you."

As Ocevia braced herself for an attack, knowing it was inevitable, Azure grabbed her hand and began pulling her away. When she turned away from their enemies, glancing in the direction they swam, Ocevia noticed a merchant ship moving toward them. The moment they reached a rock outcropping running along the channel, they began to sing, their voices blending perfectly into the song they knew would speak to the souls of the sailors. Oona and Lucia could barely be heard over the storm, but Ocevia could see them singing across the channel. Aiming to outshine the bloodthirsty pair, Ocevia and Azure sang louder, hoping to catch the ship's attention before their enemies got to them first.

Come to me,
your long-lost love,
and hold me in your arms.
The gods above,
and the goddess below,
brought me back to you.

As the ship veered in their direction, the two mermaids hid behind the rocks, singing their haunting song as they did every night. Their voices rose above the howling wind, echoing through the darkness as if bewitching the ship. In turbulent waters, the craft floated as if there was no captain, toward the rocks that would crush its bow and send it to the depths. The sailors were mesmerized by their song, becoming disoriented and losing control of their vessel.

The ship crashed into the jagged rocks as Ocevia watched, causing a loud sound that echoed throughout the night. A thunderous bolt of lightning boomed overhead, creating an ominous beat to the sounds of crunching wood and victims' screams.

No matter how many years passed, Ocevia could not forget the piercing wails of the dying. She was haunted by them in her dreams. Despite her guilt, she and Azure would share the souls they recovered from the shipwreck as they always have. The task of collecting souls on board would not be easy, however. The fight was inevitable with Oona and Lucia across the channel. Although Azure and

Ocevia's song caused the crash, Oona would not let them take credit for all the lives lost.

"I'm going to head for the stern to see how many are already in the water," Ocevia said just before she swam away.

Swimming around the back of the ship, Ocevia sang to lure the sailors away from anything that could keep them afloat. Ocevia wasn't surprised when her friend didn't follow. Getting Azure to the channel and forcing her to crash ships was all she could handle. It was why her back had more lines carved into it than the cave wall. If she had done what the others did and approached the ships with the intention of drowning everyone on board, more souls would have been removed from her debt, but she could not do so. Guilt and the need to fight against her captor kept Azure hidden in the shadows even as Ocevia took the light from those who succumbed to the sea, sacrificing them to the Sea Goddess.

After every soul had entered the sea, their lives extinguished, Ocevia expected Oona and Lucia to start trouble. She also expected Azure to find her among the wreckage, but as Ocevia swam around the pieces of debris, her friend was not there, nor were their enemies. She was completely alone in the storm.

After swimming through the turbulent sea for hours, Ocevia was exhausted and still couldn't find Azure. The thought that something had happened to her friend weighed heavily on her mind, but she didn't know where else to look. With the shifting current, she could no longer smell Azure's scent on the water. Although Ocevia's stomach clenched, she had no other option but to return to their cave and hope Azure was there. If not, she would have to wait until daylight and search for her again. Mermaids may have had the ability to see in the dark, but the storm made it nearly impossible.

When the large island darkened the sky before her, Ocevia was disheartened to see no bonfire burning, hinting that Azure was probably not there. There were endless places she could have gone, chased off by the storm, or by their enemies. She could have sought shelter on another one of the islands that were scattered throughout the Lamalis Sea. Ocevia knew Azure could handle herself. Despite this, her chest felt heavy with unease. Even as she climbed up onto the rocks and shifted into her legs, she couldn't shake the feeling that something wasn't right. She had a pressing sense of dread, as if a storm was brewing in the distance and she was in its path. She looked around, searching for some sign of impending danger, but she could find none.

Although she saw no obvious threat, the feeling of unease persisted, her pounding heart seeming to know something she didn't.

In place of lighting a fire and trying to fall asleep, Ocevia transformed back into her tail and leapt into the sea, heading toward the place where she'd last seen her friend.

CHAPTER 5

DARKNESS ON THE HORIZON

After swimming for hours, Ocevia did not find her friend, and she did not sense her on the water. Wherever Azure was, she wasn't in the sea anymore, unless she was locked away in the palace, a thought Ocevia quickly pushed away. Although she didn't know if Oona and Lucia took Azure, she knew it was likely. Oona was enraged after Azure yelled at her in the channel. Even so, Ocevia knew she would be thrown into the dungeons if she ventured into the palace grounds without being invited. She would never find her friend if she was locked away. Her only option was to wait and see if Azure appeared.

For a few days, at least. After a few days, if her friend didn't return, she would reevaluate going to the palace.

Returning to the small island where they spent most of their days, Ocevia waited for Azure to come back. She kept herself busy with menial activities, setting fires and eating fish, carving into the cave wall and watching the sea for signs of her missing friend. Since she had no other option, she hunted every night, but she focused more on finding Azure than collecting souls. They'd been inseparable since Azure took the bargain and entered the sea. They were like sisters to each other. She wouldn't abandon Ocevia without an explanation.

On the fourth day, Ocevia realized she needed to move. She no longer expected Azure to return to the cave after being absent for so many days. Still, she wasn't ready to give up. She couldn't give up hope. Instead of waiting on land, she decided to wait below the surface, where she could sense Azure as soon as she reentered the water.

Shifting back into her mermaid form, Ocevia slid off the rocks and back into the deep blue sea, ignoring the storm that loomed on the horizon. It would not bother her if she was in the depths. She took one last look back at the shore, lightning sending crawling fingers of light across the sky in the distance.

With a flick of her tail, she dove beneath the waves, the salty tang of the ocean filling her senses. She surrendered to the increasing current, her worries intensifying as the depths enveloped her. The Lamalis Sea was a dangerous environment, with places where mermaids could hide, but also places where they could become injured or be taken. Besides pirates, there were creatures sent by other gods

that posed more risks than even Ocevia could have imagined. She saw Azure in every scenario in her head as she
swam, no matter how hard she tried to push the images
away.

Submerged beneath the surface, she swam swiftly toward the bottom when the scent of Oona and Lucia chilled
her blood. They were nearby.

As she hid behind coral in a small underwater cave,
she hoped the evil mermaids wouldn't notice her. Even
though she couldn't hear them, it was obvious they were
up to something. She held her breath and waited, her
heart pounding in her ears. There was no doubt in her
mind that they were searching for the same thing as she
was: the missing mermaid. The fact that they didn't have
Azure was a relief, but she still had to find Azure before
they did, and she had no idea where to look.

While remaining in the shadows, Ocevia swam just
below the surface, doing her best to keep Oona and Lucia
in her sights. A storm swept over them as they swam,
obscuring the sky. The more the stormy sea churned and
swirled around her, the more difficult it was for her to
keep up. She battled the powerful waves until her entire
body hurt, but she only swam harder. Something told her
that if she lost them, she would never find her friend.

Just when she thought they must have realized she
was following them and they were leading her away on
purpose, an enormous rock island appeared in the distance. Ocevia watched as Oona and Lucia continued to
move closer to the island, peeking over the surface as they
climbed onto the rocky shore. Crawling across the ground,

they shifted into their legs but stayed low as though not to be seen.

The back of Ocevia's tongue burned as dread rose in her throat. Nothing happened for several long moments. Oona and Lucia didn't move. Instead, they remained crouched behind the brush in the forested area on the edge of the island, staring in the direction of the caves.

The obscured view prevented Ocevia from seeing what they were seeing, so she swam to the side to get a better view. When Ocevia lifted her eyes again, as if their prize was finally emerging from the caves, Oona and Lucia jumped out from behind the brush, darting out of sight again.

Ducking beneath the surface, she swam closer until she was almost at the shore. Her gaze peered above the water just in time to see the evil mermaids confronting a human man. He lifted his sword toward them, ready to fight, just as Azure's aroma met Ocevia's nose.

CHAPTER 6

RELEASING THE MONSTER

Heavy rains made it difficult for Ocevia to see what was happening beyond the beach as the storm intensified. She could still smell her friend on the water, but if Azure was nearby, she was hiding herself well.

With his sword in hand, the human man glared at the two mermaids, but he didn't move forward to attack. Neither did they. All three were at a standstill, the rain filling the air with heavy silence. Ocevia was unsure of what to do, her mind racing as she tried to think of a way to save him without any bloodshed.

One thing that caught Ocevia off guard was how he seemed unsurprised that the two females had arrived seemingly out of nowhere. He seemed to be expecting them, which confirmed her suspicions that Azure was with him. Confusion filled her with the same thoughts however, because she didn't understand what her friend would be doing with a human man. Azure knew that relations with humans were forbidden and saving him versus sacrificing him to the sea would only land her in chains.

It only took a moment for realization to hit Ocevia, however, and dread threatened to consume her. If Azure had saved the man from the ship they'd sank, for whatever reason, and had brought him here, it would explain why Oona and Lucia had hunted them down. If that was the case, she knew her friend and the man would not leave the island alive.

Oona lifted her hands to the sky, threatening to unleash the powers she'd earned through lifetimes of service to the Sea Goddess if he did not comply. However, he stood strong. He was stalling.

"I've already told you. I don't know who she is. I'm here alone," he called out, his voice firm and unafraid. He was protecting her friend. Azure had to have been the female he was talking about, but Ocevia still didn't understand.

"Lies!" Oona roared as she scanned their surroundings for signs of Azure, her voice laced with disdain. The mer-bitches hated humans. It was one of the reasons they were able to kill without remorse. Ocevia followed her enemy's eyes, but her friend was nowhere to be found.

For a few heartbeats, nothing happened. Suddenly, as those on the beach stood at an impasse, a dagger flew from the tree line, the blade striking Oona in the shoulder.

The evil mermaid screamed as she hit the ground, clutching her shoulder as blood spurted from the wound. Oona was injured, but Ocevia knew it would not keep her down for long. She had the power to heal herself.

As the injured mermaid lay sprawled on the ground, her eyes staring into the forest as she looked for Azure, the man behind her ran for Lucia. Using his sword, he knocked the dagger out of the other mermaid's hand and grabbed it off the ground as his opponent lunged for it. Unlike Oona, Lucia was like a feral animal, much less able to control her instincts than her friend.

"I'm going to get you for that, human!" she growled, her teeth bared as her matted blond hair swung around her face.

Turning away from him for a moment, Lucia darted to her injured friend, pulling the dagger from her shoulder as blood continued to pour onto the ground. Ocevia bit her lip as she treaded water, needing to come up with a plan to help him before one of the mermaids killed him. Nothing short of death would stop them if Miris had sent them to collect his soul and capture her rebel mermaid. He was running out of time.

Even though Oona was clearly still injured, she rose onto shaky legs, turning to look toward the forest, where she thought Azure was hiding. In the background, the human man and Lucia circled each other, each with a weapon in hand and ready to fight. Following Oona's line of sight, Ocevia sought to find her friend. The clanging of blades drew her eyes back to where Lucia had her legs wrapped around the human man, holding him pinned to the ground. Although he was much larger than Lucia, the rabid mermaid possessed supernatural strength. Snarling, she ripped free from his arms and tried to grasp his throat as he reached for a blade that was several feet away.

In the chaos unfolding before her, Ocevia watched another dagger fly, barely missing Oona, who ducked just in time to avoid it.

Ocevia scanned the forest again, her heart beating like a war drum inside her, screaming for her to act, but she couldn't locate her friend. The thoughts strumming through her mind could have catastrophic consequences, so she couldn't act without making sure Azure was somewhere safe.

A cruel smile spreading across her face, Oona spun around with her weapon at hand. Behind her, Lucia restrained the human man beneath her as they both struggled to reach the blade.

"I know you're there, Azure." Oona's tone was one of disdain and sheer arrogance. As she smirked toward the forest, Azure wasn't visible in the dense foliage, at least Ocevia couldn't see her. Oona kept her eyes toward the forest, the struggle behind her halting when Lucia grasped the bloody dagger she'd pulled from Oona's shoulder off the ground and pressed it against the human's throat.

"Show yourself, or we'll kill your lover boy." Oona glanced over her healing shoulder, at the man pinned beneath her friend. As the skin slowly knitted back together, a smirk played on her lips. "Not that we won't kill him, anyway, I mean." She chuckled. "He's basically already a dead man."

Laughing, Lucia spit on the ground beside his head. Despite thrashing his legs and trying to force the violent mermaid off, he could not knock her off him. Ocevia stiffened as she watched Lucia press the blade harder against his throat, relieved when it didn't break the skin.

As Ocevia scanned the beach again, Azure stepped out of the brush, making her breath seize in her lungs. "If I surrender, you have to let him go," Azure said with conviction.

Bile rose in Ocevia's throat as the story seemed to unfold in her mind. In saving the life of a human, her friend acted against Miris' rules, and her life would be forfeited for it.

Using her blade to clean her fingernails, Oona looked bored. "I don't know, Azure. Our Goddess would be quite angry if we set him free. His soul belongs to her."

Knowing she needed to do something, *anything*, Ocevia pulled the seashell necklace off her neck as rage and fear bubbled inside her. She was terrified of the beast hiding inside the unassuming piece of jewelry, but she pushed those fears aside. All that mattered was saving her friend, and she couldn't do that with her most lethal form left contained.

Unleashed power surged through Ocevia's veins, the force of it pulling a silent scream from her mouth as she sank deeper into the depths. As though on instinct, she threw her arms out, calling upon the ancient power of the kraken to unleash its wrath upon her enemies.

Midnight-colored water churned around her, Ocevia's tiny body twisting and stretching as eight rust-colored tentacles replaced her delicate arms. Her beautiful face, almost too gentle to be a killer, morphed into a massive head with a dozen feelers coming from its snout. A roar ripped from the beast as decades of restrained power begged for a way out, the sound making the sea tremble as the weight of her changed form pulled her to the sea floor.

Remembering how her inability to control the beast within had led to her being taken away from her family, grief overwhelmed her. Her failure to control the monster had prompted her mother to make the deal for her life in the first place, sending her away forever. It was her family's job to protect her, to love her no matter what, and they had thrown her away, allowing her to be cursed to a life of loneliness and devastation. The pain of this memory only fueled her rage. She wanted to destroy, *to kill*, until it eased the torturous emotions inside of her, but she couldn't.

Twisting in the direction of the surface, she forced her scattered mind to focus. Azure and the human man needed saving. If she was too late, then releasing her ancient curse had been for nothing.

With the storm darkening the sky, the monstrous creature Ocevia had become crashed through the surface, her mind still disoriented from the transformation. Massive tentacles thrashed around her, threatening destruction, but she aimed her reach toward the island, zeroing in on Oona.

Before her enemy had a chance to react, Ocevia wrapped one deadly appendage around her enemy, rows of suction cups preventing the evil mermaid from slipping away. Though futile, Oona thrashed in her grip, jabbing her dagger into the tentacle that was larger than three of her.

In the final moments before Ocevia's bulbous head plum-
meted back below the surface, she saw her best friend's

horror-filled eyes as she watched Ocevia's greatest secret
come to life.

CHAPTER 7

BLACK BLOOD

A s Ocevia spiraled down toward the sea floor with Oona so slight in her tentacles, memories of Azure's terrified eyes plagued her mind. She knew Azure didn't know it was truly her inside the massive body, but she also knew the secret would one day be revealed. When that day came, she realized her friend would be just as afraid of her as her family had been. If Azure shunned her too, it would break her heart.

The chaos of the kraken's mind clouded her own, centuries of memories that passed down from one being to the next. No matter how hard she tried to focus on one thought, it got swept up in the typhoon and warped into something else. Even as she tried to pull her friend back into her mind, a jab of Oona's dagger into the appendage holding the mermaid demanded her attention. Black blood mixed with the dark water around them as Ocevia jerked her tentacle to the side. As she reached around with another limb, smacking the dagger out of her captive's hand, Oona's legs shifted into a tail, allowing her to slip free.

Not used to the bulky body of a giant cephalopod, her enemy moved away quicker than she expected. Oona slung her arms behind her as her tail pushed her forward, throwing a bolt of power at the kraken, trying to slow the beast down, but Ocevia dropped out of the way.

Where Ocevia lacked in speed, she made up with size. Circling around, her tentacles surged out behind her, propelling her like lightning after the fleeing mermaid. She made up the distance in mere moments, slamming into Oona with the force of a tidal wave as her momentum was too great to stop.

Knocked unconscious, the mermaid's body crumpled, her black hair billowing behind her like a jar of spilled ink as she sank toward the coral below.

Burning rage, a hunger for destruction, sent the kraken toward the injured mermaid, instead of back to the surface to check on her friend. She knew Lucia may still be on the island, but Ocevia was not yet strong enough to fight the instincts that ruled her unleashed form.

After taking one hesitant glance toward the surface, she turned her turquoise eyes to the darkness below, following Oona's scent on the current to where she'd fallen.

Swimming as fast as she could toward her kill, Ocevia's conscience battled her bloodlust– that, and Miris' wrath.

She knew if she killed the Sea Goddess' most trusted servant, she would face certain death. Still, the horrors that haunted Ocevia's dreams, the things that she'd done, were only a shadow in the mind of her in the form of the kraken. The creature may have been a part of her, but its power was ancient, and her fears were merely a grain of sand in the sea surrounding it.

The figure of a mermaid appeared among the seaweed and sand when Ocevia finally made it to the bottom of the Lamalis Sea. Oona regained consciousness as the kraken's power circulated around her, lifting her arms as she attempted to summon the power Miris had gifted her, that which could squeeze the life from her enemy's body. Before she'd had a chance to take one heartbeat from the beast, two tentacles reached toward her, wrapping around her outstretched arms. As their eyes met, even with the knowing look of horror in the mermaid's face, there was no hesitation when the tentacles ripped Oona apart.

Blood colored the water crimson as its metallic taste entered Ocevia's snout, her feelers spreading out and taking in all it could. The kraken savored it, hungered for it.

Taking one last look at the fallen enemy in the sand, a momentary thought entered Ocevia's mind, making its way through the chaos. She had to get to her friend.

With a thrust of her tentacles below her, she surged toward the island. Before she could see the surface, however, a flash of pain from one of her tentacles forced her attention to shift.

Ocevia bellowed, cartwheeling her body as a pressure wrapped around the burning appendage. The figure of a mermaid, blond hair streaming above her head like fire, clung to a tentacle, trying to sever it with a sword, vengeance clear in her eyes

Like a human with a parasite, the monster flailed against its attacker, swinging its other tentacles around it as it tried to knock Lucia off. The mermaid looked up at her, a scowl on her rabid face as she stabbed the sword into the limb again, sending black blood pouring into the sea around them. With another cry of pain, Ocevia slammed one of her uninjured limbs into Lucia, catapulting her into the depths below.

Ocevia tried to swim toward the surface, but every movement of her body was laced with pain as her injury bled unchecked. Grasping the seashell necklace tightly in the suction of one of her tentacles, she lost consciousness, the energy to fuel the beast draining as she drifted toward the darkness below.

When Ocevia regained consciousness, the sand and sea-weed beneath her strewn body cushioning her like a soft bed, but something was wrong. She couldn't breathe, but before she could understand why, pain burned through her lower half.

A garbled scream left her lips as she turned toward her tail, bubbles leaving her mouth as she gagged on the water entering her throat. She was a mermaid. She could breathe underwater, but when she looked down toward her tail, there were legs instead. A deep gash spanned the width of her pale thigh, spilling red blood into the water. When she'd lost the energy to keep the kraken form, she'd shifted back into a human.

Panic icing her veins, she flailed her arms, closing her lips as tight as she could to keep the breath from leaving her lungs as she moved her arms in a desperate attempt to get to the surface. Ocevia tried to shift back into a mermaid, but her body didn't respond to her pleas, the pain and lack of energy too great to overcome. If she didn't make it back to the beach, she would drown.

Please. Please Please. Using every ounce of life she had left, Ocevia begged no one as she used her arms and legs to swim to the surface, clenching her teeth as pain threatened to pull her into the darkness again. Just when she thought she wouldn't make it, that she would die on the current like so many souls she'd cursed to the same fate, her lungs filled with salty night air.

In the darkness of night, her fingers clawed into the sandy beach, dragging her out of the water. She choked and sputtered as she tried to recover her breathing. The beach was silent. There were no footsteps running to greet her, no sign of her best friend or the human male. With nothing but moonlit darkness around her, and trees swaying in the breeze, Ocevia laid her face on the sand, and closed her eyes.

Although she tried to let sleep consume her, pain wracked her body again and she cried out. If she didn't find help, even with her accelerated healing abilities as a mermaid, she knew she would die. Shifting into the monster had drained her power, making even her ability to heal herself difficult.

Gritting her teeth, she dug her fingers into the sand, pulling the dead weight of her body forward an inch at a time. Even in the dark, she knew blood still poured from the wound. It left a trail for predators to find an easy meal, if there were such beasts on the island. The fear of becoming something's dinner drove her forward, across the sand and onto the rocky ground toward the caves she knew were just ahead.

Although her powers were dimmed, and she was in pain, Ocevia couldn't mistake the scent of a burning fire when she approached the three massive caves. It led her to the two connected caves on the left. The one with the blocked entrance all the way to the end was where she knew she would find her friend.

"Azure." Her voice was merely a breath of sound she knew only she could hear. With a grunt of pain, she pulled herself to her knees, clawing at the stones that blocked her from the fire and rescue. The closer she got, the stronger the scent of them grew. Azure was inside.

"Azure. Help me."

Putting all her strength into the effort, Ocevia climbed over the largest boulder blocking the entrance and fell through the small opening she'd created, landing with a thump on the ground on the other side.

Chapter 8

FORBIDDEN ROMANCE

Lying in a heap just inside the barricaded entrance of the cave, the cold stone floor chilled Ocevia's crumpled body. The room was dark, but she didn't need to be able to see her surroundings to know Azure was close by.

"Azure?" Even speaking was a strain, but she knew her friend wouldn't know it was her in the darkness. "Azure, are you still there?"

Hurried footsteps approached her just before Azure dropped to the ground beside her, touching her arm. Her friend examined her body, but Ocevia knew Azure wouldn't see the wound with her laying on it. Groaning, she tried to stand, but she was too weak to hold her own weight, so she fell back to the ground.

"Elios... Come help her. Let's get her back to the fire," Azure called out to the human male as she smoothed Ocevia's wet hair off her face. A moment later, she was scooped up in his arms, her face falling against his bare muscled chest. He walked quickly to another location in the cave, but Ocevia's consciousness faded in and out, making it impossible to know what was happening around her.

Once he stopped walking and crouched to place her on the ground, Ocevia's eyes fluttered open. In the flickering firelight, she noticed both her friend and the human man were nude, but she didn't have the energy to analyze why.

As soon as he moved away, Azure knelt beside her, moving her hands across Ocevia's body as she looked for the injury. She knew her wound was still bleeding. The loss of blood continued to make her weaker, but every time she tried to speak, the words didn't leave her mind.

"What happened to you, Ocevia?"

The moment Azure found the gash and held pressure against it to stem the bleeding, Ocevia moaned in pain.

"I need something to staunch the bleeding." The moment the command left Azure's mouth, the sound of the male's bare feet echoed through the cave, moving further away. No longer able to endure the pain or fight the exhaustion, Ocevia fell into unconsciousness before he returned.

Dreams and reality intertwined as Ocevia's body took the rest it desperately needed. She hadn't been completely unconscious, however. Throughout her fitful state of quasi-consciousness, she could hear her friend and the human male talking, as well as sounds of them moving around the multiple rooms of the cave. It wasn't enough to know what they were doing, but knowing they were at least nearby brought her comfort.

When she finally woke up enough to open her eyes fully to look around, the cave was empty. After being carried so far by the human male the night before, she realized there were more rooms in the cave. Still, not seeing them in the room with her caused her to panic. The worry that they'd left her behind tightened her chest. Before she could remind herself that Azure would never do that to her, two silhouettes entered the cave from a narrow pathway in the stone. When Azure's eyes met hers, her friend dashed across the room, dropping to the floor.

"What happened?" Ocevia asked, her voice gravelly from sleep. Grabbing a cup of water from the ground, Azure lifted it to her lips. In her eagerness to consume too much at once, Ocevia sputtered when she tried to drink.

"I was going to ask you the same thing. You showed up with a giant gash on your leg and then passed out as we tried to stop the bleeding. You've been sleeping ever since." As Ocevia rubbed her hand down her leg, she winced when she grazed the bandages. Azure swatted Ocevia's hand away, narrowing her eyes on her. "How did you get that injury?"

Vague memories of what happened below the surface flooded into Ocevia's mind. Still in a daze from the blood loss and extreme use of energy, she ran her hands across her face and limbs, checking for more wounds. "I don't really remember much after seeing the merbitches in the water. I overheard them talking about finding you, so I followed them."

She knew she'd lied, but she wasn't ready to tell her best friend about her secret yet. The truth would come out eventually, but she needed more time. Turning to stare at the cave wall where water slowly cascaded down, Ocevia twisted her shell necklace around her throat. "I was beneath the sea when something pulled Oona in and then I was dragged into the depths during the chaos. Someone's dagger got me in the leg."

Wiping the water from Ocevia's chin, Azure leaned back on her heels. "Did they survive the attack? From the creature, I mean."

Having already lied, Ocevia shrugged and reached for the water again, taking a large gulp before leaning back on her elbows. Azure handed the empty cup to the human male, Elios, so he could refill it. "I'm not sure if they made it. I drifted to the bottom after I got hurt. It took a while for me to make it back to the surface. I had to shift and swim as a human. My tail wouldn't function properly with the gash."

Elios returned to them a moment later and handed the water back to Azure before adding another log to the fire. He seemed to be uncomfortable, or like there was a lot on his mind. When he lowered himself to the ground beside them, Ocevia realized he was handsome, with dark brown hair and brilliant blue eyes. It was also clear that he and Azure had something between them. "And who is he?"

Before responding, Azure gave her a sidelong glance. "This is Elios. I pulled him off a rock outcropping after the shipwreck and brought him here."

As Ocevia scanned Elios from head to toe, her stare almost clinical, she grinned at their near nakedness. Being a mermaid, Azure rarely covered her body, and was merely wearing strips of leather over her breasts and her bottom. Elios, however, was bare chested. A circular tattoo of a broken chain decorated one of his pectorals, and his body was chiseled from a lifetime of using a sword. If Azure was having romantic relations with the human male, even if it was forbidden, Ocevia couldn't say she blamed her. "I see. Where did you find leather?"

Huffing as she stood, Azure crossed the room and dug through a pile of fruit. When she returned, she had a mango in her hand. Having not eaten in days, Ocevia's stomach growled just at seeing it. Elios took the fruit and began to cut it into chunks with his dagger.

Soon after, Azure returned, taking a chunk of mango from him and handing it to Ocevia. "We found leather and a bunch of other materials washed up on the beach from shipwrecks. Elios and I made a raft using some of the wreckage this morning. We can't stay here now that the others have found us. We need to leave as soon as possible."

CHAPTER 9

THE THIRD WHEEL

Azure and Elios intended to leave the island, and Oce- via couldn't blame them. After being attacked by Oona and Lucia, they all realized Miris would eventually send others.

"Good plan," Ocevia said, fruit juice dribbling down her chin from the chunk of mango in her mouth. Azure laughed, but Ocevia continued to chew, knowing she was making a mess. As hungry as she was, she didn't care. "Any idea where you're headed?"

As Azure glanced at Elios, he shrugged. "We haven't discussed it, but I think you mean *we*. Looks like you're stuck with us for a while."

"I'll be fine." Not wanting to intrude on her friend's forbidden romance, Ocevia waved her hand dismissively. She tried to stand, but pain blazed up her injured leg. With a hiss, she fell back to the ground. Until she healed, she knew she would be unable to travel on her own. "On second thought, I guess I'll be a third-wheel for a while."

As Elios chuckled, Azure glared at him. A boyish grin spread across his face as he lifted sticky hands. "What?"

Rolling her eyes, Azure pointed a finger at Ocevia in a playful gesture. "Don't encourage this one. She's trouble."

Ocevia's eyes widened as she smiled sweetly, knowing it would only fluster her friend more. Between the two of them, she'd always been the more playful one. What surprised her was the obvious affection between Azure and the human man. They appeared to care about each other a lot, and to be comfortable with each other, more than she would've expected after such a short time knowing each other.

"So, when do we leave?" Despite being weak and unable to stand, Ocevia managed to maintain a sitting position with little effort. Although it still hurt, it was tolerable.

"First light," Elios said, looking up at Azure for confirmation. Her head nodded in agreement.

Their plan was to wait until first light, when most mermaids slept, hoping that those hunting them would be resting. What Ocevia knew that the others didn't was that Lucia was alive, and that filled her with icy concern. As they sat by the fire, the feral mermaid could have been waiting for them to exit the cave and kill them all.

"Yes. Today, Elios and I will gather more food and pack up any supplies we need, so we're ready to leave in the morning."

"What about me?" As Ocevia took another bite of the mango, its sticky orange juice left a trail down her forearm. Azure didn't suppress her laughter.

"Well, first, you need a bath." When Ocevia realized that Azure was calling her dirty and possibly stinky, her eyebrow arched, but she didn't interrupt her friend. In any case, it was true. "Next, you'll rest. Elios and I will paddle the raft until you're well enough to help."

Ocevia scoffed, prepared to argue, not wanting to seem helpless. "I can help. And I don't really want to climb back into the sea to bathe right now, but thanks. I don't know if you realize, but my last trek in that water was not so great. Wet my tail? Yes. Submerge in the sea? No."

Azure handed Ocevia the glass of water as she snorted. "You lost a lot of blood, so no, you aren't paddling yet. Also, we have a hot spring here."

"And you're just telling me this now?" Ocevia scowled, but her tone was mischievous. Although she had noticed the water dripping down the far wall, she hadn't seen the pool on that side of the cave. While there were hot springs scattered throughout the area, they were rare. A flutter of excitement filled her stomach.

"Sorry. I must have forgotten on account of you bleeding out and all. My mistake. It's over there." In between bites of mango, Azure gestured toward the pool.

Ocevia peered through the darkness, the fire providing the only light in the cavernous space, as the idea of a hot spring drew her interest. "You and your boyfriend have got to carry me over there. It's been so long since I've sat in a hot bath. There aren't many that we are allowed to go to."

Knowing she shouldn't walk on her injured leg, Ocevia lifted her arms, asking Elios to bring her to the pool. He did not hesitate, lifting her as though she weighed nothing and easing her down onto the stone ledge just inside the spring water.

Although there was worry that the water could irritate her wound, she slipped down into its warmth, shifting her legs into a tail with a burst of energy she didn't know she had.

The gash stung her with pain, but it was nothing she couldn't handle. If they were leaving the island, she needed to submerge her tail before they did so. Knowing Lucia had probably gone back to Miris to report her crimes, she didn't want to chance getting back into the sea. Not when her scent could be carried by the current and lead them straight to her.

Although Ocevia realized she was no longer safe in the Lamalis Sea, and that leaving with her friends was her best option, it still filled her with trepidation. It wasn't about her being forbidden from entering the human lands. After killing Oona, she was way past breaking the rules. What she was concerned about was being away from the water.

Ever since she'd become a mermaid, Miris had warned her that if she didn't submerge her tail every day, it would rot, hence killing her. She realized it could have been a lie meant to keep her where Miris wanted her, but she didn't want to take that chance. If they did go into the human lands, the further into the mountains they went, the less natural water sources they would find. Even away from the sea, she was sure they would find a way, but it still unnerved her.

As Ocevia floated in the hot water of the spring, the pool large enough for several people, Azure and Elios left the cave to gather more supplies. Even through the narrow corridor leading into the front chamber of the cave, Ocevia could tell the sun would slumber soon. They all knew not to be outside during the night. During the hours of darkness, mermaids searched the sea for souls to take, and they knew if they were being hunted, they should remain behind the blocked entrance of the cave.

Even with fear of the unknown tightening her chest, there was still a shiver of excitement in her. She hadn't been on human land since she was taken from her home at eleven years old, but she always wanted to return. It wasn't like she could search for her family if she found a way to escape Miris' clutches on land, however. She didn't even know if they would want to see her again, or if she wanted to see them. For as long as she lived, there would be a part of her that was resentful towards her parents for submitting her to a life of servitude instead of loving and protecting her.

Although her heart was hurt, a piece would always love her parents and miss them, and she would always picture them in her dreams.

Leaning against the back of the hot spring, Ocevia closed her eyes and enjoyed the way the steaming water soothed her bones. Behind her eyelids, she could see her mother, sitting beside her on the bed and telling her stories about the sea. Her blue eyes were ablaze with love, but she didn't trust the memory. Not when her mother had given her away. It was too much for Ocevia to bear the pain of her loss, and she cursed as a tear ran down her cheek.

A shuffle of footsteps returned behind her, and her two companions' voices met her ears. She tried to push away the thoughts of her family, convincing herself that life was better without them.

CHAPTER 10

SETTING SAIL

W hen they went to sleep that night, Ocevia curled up on a pallet of palm fronds next to the fire, with a strip of leather to keep her warm. Elios and Azure cuddled together on the other side of the blaze. Once they'd returned from gathering supplies from the island's forested area for their trip, including several mangos, Elios and Azure had replaced the rocks and boulders that blocked the entrance of the cave, making it look as though it was impassable.

Although Ocevia's energy had been drained enough to make it difficult to stay away, she hadn't missed the tension in her friend's face before she'd laid down for sleep.

Azure was worried about leaving the island, and Ocevia understood why. Traveling with an injured mermaid and a human man, there would be a lot of pressure on Azure's shoulders to keep them safe. There was no doubt Elios could fight, but he wasn't immortal. Neither were mermaids, but they had longer than human lifespans, and their bodies healed quickly. With the Sea Goddess undoubtedly looking for them as they traveled by mere raft across the sea, the risks were impossibly high.

Somewhere in the chaotic tumble of Ocevia's mind, the thoughts draining more energy than she had to spare, she succumbed to unconsciousness as the flames flickered in the dark space. She was still lying with her eyes closed, thinking about the permanent decisions they would be making that day, when Azure padded around the fire, her footsteps light against the stone floor only moments before Ocevia felt the tender touch of Azure touching her shoulder to wake her.

"How are you feeling, Ocevia? Any pain?" Ocevia pulled on primitive shoes made from salvaged materials as Azure folded their leather blankets. Having not worn shoes since childhood, the flimsy material gave her the impression that it would be more trouble than it was worth. If she had to run, she preferred running barefoot instead of with straps tied to her feet. Giving one last tug on the straps, she tightened the pieces to hold them as securely as possible. "We'll have to find a way to get us proper shoes before we start our hike into the mountains."

Before carrying their packs into the cave's front chamber, Elios stopped to kiss Azure. With a mischievous grin, Ocevia smirked. She intended to tease her friend later, but she felt a heavy sense of longing as she watched them. She had never thought love was possible, not while enslaved to the Sea Goddess. Seeing Azure and Elios together, she realized she wanted love more than anything, even more than her freedom from the sea, more than her family. It fluttered her heart with hope at the thought that she might find love in the human world, just like her friend had. Despite knowing it would be difficult, she was determined to escape the Sea Goddess. Having been a slave most of her life, she wanted to experience love, and she was prepared to do whatever it took to make that happen. "I have credits in Avrearyn and Ceveasea. You can get whatever you want."

Seeing him leave, Ocevia's eyebrows shot up, and Azure shook her head. "No. We are not going on a shopping spree with his coin," Azure said before sticking her tongue out at Ocevia, who made a silly face right back. Having her friend around, knowing she was safe, had allowed Ocevia to once again be herself. It was a good feeling.

Leaving Ocevia's side, Azure lifted a sack of leather blankets and headed after Elios. Once they left the back chamber of the cave, heading into the corridor that would take them into the large front room and then the blocked exit, Ocevia could only hear their muffled voices. She did not follow behind them, needing to slide on the strips of leather that would serve as clothing, but light streamed into the cave a moment later as they moved the boulders blocking the entrance so they could take the raft out.

Several minutes later, as Ocevia leaned against the wall of the cave while she waited to walk to the raft, Azure and Elios returned. She moved to walk forward, but before she made it more than two stumbling steps, hissing through her teeth as the pain of her injury shot fire down her leg, Elios wrapped his arms around her and lifted her like an infant.

"Put. Me. Down. Please. I can walk, Elios." Ocevia knew her words were clipped, and that he was only trying to help, but she didn't care. After more than a day of them taking care of her, she was ready to take care of herself. She realized she was being prideful, but Elios was not her lover anyway. He had no obligation to take care of her.

"Not until we get you to the raft. It took a long time to get your bleeding to stop and I can tell it still hurts," he responded, holding tightly onto her as he continued to walk toward the beach.

Walking beside them, Azure added, "We can tell it still hurts you, Ocevia. Just wait another day to walk on it."

She struggled a bit more, flailing her limbs to try to get comfortable, but eventually gave up as they approached the raft.

With pieces of crashed ships and wood from the forest fastened together with bits of leather and a torn sail, Ocevia was glad she could swim. She knew it was the best they were able to build, and it appeared large enough for the three of them to travel in, albeit cramped, but it did not seem stable. All she could hope was that they didn't meet a storm, or the mermaids hunting for them. If they kept their scents out of the water, however, the mermaids would have a hard time finding them.

"You know," Ocevia started as Elios set her down in the raft, "I'm never going to strengthen my leg if you don't let me try."

His eyes narrowed as he pushed the raft into the water. "You can practice when we're in Avrearyn. We need to get out of here while it's still early."

As Ocevia crossed her arms across her chest and pouted, Azure smirked. As the raft floated in the shallows, Elios held it steady while Azure climbed inside, a paddle in her hand. Moving to the front of the craft, Azure stuck the long paddle into the water, holding it as still as she could, allowing Elios to climb into the rear. A moment later, using a long board, he pushed them away from the shore and out to sea.

CHAPTER 11

TO FREEDOM

S imilarly to the day before, Ocevia's energy waned, pulling her into unconsciousness repeatedly. Both Azure and Elios paddled when the wind was not in their favor, maneuvering the raft toward the continent. They would aim for the kingdom of Avrearyn, according to Elios. There, Elios would be able to purchase clothing and supplies from the tavern's owner and get a room for the night. They planned to buy horses and travel inland to the city of Ceveasea after resting for a night. Despite not knowing much about Elios, it was clear he had traveled extensively throughout the human world. Ocevia didn't know what he was doing in his travels, but she was curious.

Ocevia had left the human world at a young age and didn't know where they could find safety, but Elios had told her that a former slave king led a kingdom deep in the mountains. It was a place they could go for sanctuary, one where Miris might not find them.

Although the Sea Goddess prohibited her mermaids from exploring human lands, she would still send scouts to search for them. Elios was her soul to claim, and two of her mermaids acted against her wishes. As cruel as she was beautiful, Miris was vengeful, and she would not let them remain unpunished. Despite the warmth of the sun and the gentle rocking of the craft, Ocevia's throat burned with fear as she drifted off to sleep.

A gentle touch to Ocevia's shoulder pulled her out of unconsciousness just as the sun set, painting the sky in a brilliant array of pastel colors against the horizon. Although she'd slept for hours, her body was still weak. Unleashing the beast trapped in the enchanted seashell around her neck used up more energy than expected, more than she could afford. After seeing the terror she could inflict in that form, she hoped never to become that monster again.

"We should wet our tails before the sun sets," Azure said as she rubbed Ocevia's shoulder. She nodded, sliding to sit up in the cramped space.

With the wind blowing towards the continent, tension pressed against the small sail. Still, Elios pushed them forward with his paddle. When night fell, mermaids searched the sea for souls. While they weren't near the main channel where most mermaids hunted, that didn't mean no one was looking for them. It was risky for them to enter the water to wet their tails. If any mermaids were close enough, they would be able to smell them in the water. Even so, Ocevia knew she had to moisten her tail in order to avoid rot. It may have been a lie Miris told to control them, but neither was willing to take the risk.

Draping her legs over the raft's side, Ocevia slid into the cool water, mustering barely enough energy to shift into her tail. As the saltwater stung her wounds, Ocevia clenched her teeth, but the tension eased as the warm water embraced her. She couldn't stay in the water for long, but it was where she felt most at home.

"How long will it take us to reach land?"

Within moments, Azure dropped into the water beside her.

Her friend's eyes never left Elios, even as she tipped her head back to rinse her hair. Their gazes were filled with so much affection, a love that neither Ocevia nor her friend could have imagined for themselves. The romance was forbidden, but it was real. Although Ocevia hadn't discussed it with her friend, it was clear Azure and Elios shared a deep connection. A heartfelt sigh escaped Ocevia's lips as she looked away, longing for a love like theirs.

"If the wind continues to blow us toward Starspell," Elios said, "We should get there by tomorrow afternoon."

A surge of excitement sped up Ocevia's heartbeat as she climbed back into the raft, careful not to tip it over. The coastal Avrearyn city of Starspell had always intrigued her, even as a child, although she had never visited it. Stepping out of the sea and onto the continent would give her hope for freedom, for a future. The only thing they had to do was get there safely.

After climbing back into the raft, Ocevia curled up on the floor, cuddling with a leather blanket, as Elios and Azure rowed the craft, even as the wind pressed on the sail. If their scent had traveled on the water to any prowling mermaids, they would have no hope of escaping, so moving quickly away from where they'd entered the water was their top priority.

When Ocevia woke for a bit in the evening to eat, she fell quickly back to sleep, exhaustion still weighing her down. Maybe it was because she was safe in the presence of her friends, but she gave into the unconsciousness that was so insistent. If Azure hadn't been on the island to tend to her wounds and watch over her while she recovered, Ocevia realized she probably would be dead. They'd saved each other, but Ocevia still owed her friend her life.

Squinting against the sunlight, Ocevia awoke to land on the horizon, the warmth of her excitement energizing her body to remain awake.

"We're almost there, ladies," Elios said, a warm grin on his face as Azure turned to look at him. When their gazes met, their affection for each other was undeniable.

Turning away, Ocevia gazed at the approaching harbor. Mountains in the background framed a row of wooden and stone structures facing the sea. It was still too far off to see the people, but Ocevia smiled as longing filled her. Longing for love, for a normal life, a family. There were so many things she never thought she would ever have, that now seemed possible with the land close enough to touch.

"I haven't been to the human lands in a very long time. Not since I was a child. I don't remember what it was like."

Movement behind her caught Ocevia's attention and she turned around to see Azure had shifted into her mermaid form. Her tail nearly filled the raft, the iridescent violet scales reflecting the light of the sun in a kaleidoscope of colors.

"We should wet our tails before we reach land. Who knows how long it will be before we can do it again?" Azure reached into a bag, pulling out two glass bottles and filling them with water before handing one to Ocevia. As soon as Ocevia took the bottle, Azure began pouring the water on her tail, using her hand to spread the moisture across the surface. "I don't want to attempt getting in the water again. It'll draw attention if we flip the raft so close to the shore, not to mention spreading our scents. We'll have to do our best by wetting them from here."

As Ocevia nodded, she shifted into mermaid form, making the vessel even more crowded. As they collected water in the glass bottles and rinsed their tails, Elios watched them as he paddled, eyes wide. Although revealing who they were to humans was also forbidden, she knew he'd seen Azure's mermaid form before. Azure saved him from the depths, after all. Though she didn't understand why her friend had done it, Ocevia couldn't bring herself to think that she would have done anything differently.

Throughout her years of enslavement, luring thousands of souls to the deep, Ocevia had never looked into their faces. She didn't want them to haunt her dreams. They still did, however, as shadowed silhouettes in the darkness, screaming as their lights were snuffed out. If she ever had a chance to break the cycle, knowing she could get away with it- if she ever found a male she could fall in love with and escape with- there was no doubt in Ocevia's mind that she would take that chance as well.

As Ocevia poured the salty water along her tail, wincing when it slid across her still-healing wound, her eyes were drawn to Azure and Elios and their wordless flirtation. She grinned to herself, the awkwardness of being there as their relationship blossomed making her wish to disappear to give them privacy. The raft was small, Ocevia mere inches away from Azure as her friend dampened her tail slowly, Elios' blue eyes tracking the movement of her hand like he wished to trace it with his tongue. Ocevia had never been touched by a male, or by anyone for that matter. However, the sensation of a tightening low in her belly told her she desired it badly. She didn't desire Elios, but she needed to be touched. When she ventured into the human lands, she hoped to make that happen. She wanted someone to look at her the way the handsome man paddling their raft looked at her friend. She wanted to feel the warmth of fingers on her skin, and to be looked at in a way that made her feel desired and seen.

With an internal cringe, Ocevia interrupted Azure's seductive show beside her. "Just for the record... I am not sharing a room with you two lovebirds."

Azure buried her face in her hands, embarrassment coloring her cheeks as Elios chuckled. With a stifled laugh, Ocevia drained the remaining water onto her tail and shifted back into her legs. The land was drawing ever closer, so she needed to appear human. Taking a breath, Ocevia smiled at Azure before turning her attention toward the approaching land. In the distance, she could see the docks and the bustling port beyond. Her heart raced, nervousness and excitement filling her as she braced herself for the coming journey.

While they had intended to arrive in Starspell by midday, an opposing wind delayed their arrival until just after sunset. Despite the darkness, the city bustled. Like its namesake, a million stars glinted in the deep blue sky, accentuating the endless mountain peaks. Candlelight illuminated nearly every window, revealing the silhouettes of those inside. Many people walked up and down the main street, visiting shops or returning to their homes. As Ocevia watched them live their lives in such a way, she was filled with wonder. In her heart, she longed for such a life, a life she had been denied.

"My friend's tavern is close to the harbor." Elios' voice broke through Ocevia's thoughts. "So, once we dock this contraption and gather our things, we'll go straight there. He can arrange for clothing to be brought to the tavern for us, and we can order food and drinks. It'll be comfortable there."

Nodding, Ocevia returned her eyes to the slowly approaching city. Thoughts of visiting a tavern and tasting ale for the first time, eating human food, and sleeping in a real bed filled her with giddiness. The more she imagined what it would be like, the more excitement showed on her face. The sounds of the city filled her ears as they drew closer. There was festive music coming from somewhere along what was probably the main street, probably from one of the taverns. As she tapped along to the tune, Ocevia was flooded with memories of music from her childhood, a sense of nostalgia that made her heart ache.

With her heart full and eyes shining with anticipation, she smiled. After all these years, she'd finally returned to the human lands, and the feeling of homecoming was overwhelming.

It had taken her many miles to get here, and her journey was just beginning. She had no idea what the future held, but she was ready to embrace it.

Taking a deep breath as Elios tied the raft to one of the small floating docks, Ocevia stepped off the craft and onto the wooden platform.

CHAPTER 12

STARSPELL

A s they stepped onto the docks, the makeshift raft tied to one of the pilings although they never intended to use it again, Ocevia breathed a sigh of relief. Pain still radiated from the wound in her thigh, but it had lessened significantly after all the rest she'd gotten over the past few days. She went to step forward, but before she made it more than a few steps, strong arms scooped her up as Elios lifted her like a baby. Knowing he wouldn't put her down even if she begged, she didn't bother. With Azure by their side, the trio made their way toward the strip of buildings along the main street.

As they approached the stone structure, the music from inside became louder. Even in her grumpy state, not wanting to be carried as though she couldn't take care of herself, she couldn't help but to smile as the scent of food and the sounds of revelry met her ears. The fluttering in her stomach only increased when Azure opened the heavy metal door, allowing her and Elios to enter before her.

Before she'd left the human lands, Ocevia had been too young to visit a tavern. She could vaguely picture what they'd looked like in Thatia, like a fuzzy memory that could be just her imagination, but it remained in the back of her mind as she took in the inviting space.

It was clear that the tavern must have had a good reputation in the area, as it was crowded with people seemingly enjoying their time there. Several long tables were occupied by patrons, a flurry of conversation filling the space. A few bards sang lively melodies in the corner, and the smell of freshly cooked food wafted through the air. The atmosphere was filled with cheer and excitement, as if everyone was at home with friends and family. Even the bar stools were occupied. Ocevia realized she was quite underdressed, with strips of leather over her breasts and below her waist. Still, her head was on a swivel as she took everything in, wanting desperately for Elios to put her down so she could explore and touch everything.

The bartender with short silver hair, hazel eyes, and a kind face caught Elios' attention. The tall, slender man looked to be in his middle years, maybe forty or fifty, and was talking to an elderly man with an eye patch. After meeting Elios' gaze, he left the bar, approaching them before they could make it through the crowd.

"Elios," the silver-haired man said as he approached, patting Elios on the shoulder hard enough to jolt Ocevia in his arms. She grumbled to be put down again, and this time he listened, setting her on the ground beside him. Although her legs were still weak, she stood on her own two feet, slipping into the background to stand beside Azure.

Smiling, Elios shook the man's hand. It was clear they knew each other well. "Vasso. Good to see you, old friend. Business looks like it's going well."

The older male, Vasso, smiled back, the gesture filled with warmth as he wrapped his arm around Elios' broad shoulders and turned him to look at the crowd.

"We're just passing through. Probably won't stay more than the night."

As though there was some secret knowledge between them, Vasso nodded. "Off the record it is. One room or two?"

Ocevia's stomach dropped slightly, unsure what the two males knew that she and Azure didn't. Not knowing what Elios did for a living, all she could hope was that he was an honorable person who wasn't setting them up. He seemed trustworthy, seemed like he loved her friend, but Ocevia didn't have enough experience with humans to know any better.

"Two, but near each other, if possible. We need supplies as well. My companions will need clothes, and we need something to eat. We have, unfortunately, had to travel with not much more than the clothes on our backs. Are my credits still adequate?"

Beside her, Azure wrapped her arms around her chest to hide her near nakedness. As a mermaid, they were used to wearing very little, but everyone else in the tavern was fully dressed.

Patting Elios on the shoulder again, the elderly male smiled. "Your credits are plenty. Let me grab those keys for you, and you can get these ladies settled upstairs. I'll have food and beverages brought up while Chryssa rustles up some clothes for them. The stores are closed at this hour, but she should be able to scrounge up a few things until morning."

A moment later, Vasso walked away, heading back toward the bar as Elios moved closer to them, slipping his hand into Azure's. They stood there for a few minutes, Ocevia gazing over the crowd as the band played a happy melody that had people clapping along. Her leather-wrapped foot tapped on the wooden floor, her attention wholly on the band as Vasso returned to them with two silver keys in his hand. With a lift of his hand, he led them toward the stairway nearly hidden in shadows in the back of the cabin. Elios let go of Azure's hand and wrapped his arm around Ocevia, although she objected, shouldering some of her weight as they left the tavern and climbed the darkened stairs to the inn on the second level.

The corridor on the second level was heavily shadowed, with only the light from a few sconces to illuminate it. It was clear Elios had been there before, however, and he found their guest rooms quickly, approaching the last door on the right. He turned to Ocevia as he unlocked it. "Make yourself comfortable. One of us will come to knock when Vasso sends up food and clothing. Get some rest. There are usually towels in the bathing room, and there is a bathtub for your tail."

The moment the word bathtub hit her ears, Ocevia perked up, excited to get back into the water. Moving past them, she darted into the candlelit room, throwing the door closed behind her. There was nothing more they needed to say. Elios and Azure needed their privacy, and she needed to get back in the water.

Bypassing the large bed as she shuffled through the room, the open door of the bathing room and the copper tub inside caught her eye. Her stomach grumbled with the need for food, especially after smelling the aromas in the tavern, but while she waited for dinner to be brought to her, she fully intended to soak in the tub. The problem was, as Ocevia approached the tub with a gleam of excitement in her eyes, she realized she didn't know how to operate it.

Biting down on her lip as she scratched at her cheek and looked around, she debated finding Azure to help her. That thought was quickly scratched, however, not wanting to interrupt whatever Azure and Elios were probably already engaged in. She reached for the cool metal handle and tried to twist it first. When that didn't work, she pushed and then lifted, causing something within the wall to rumble. A moment later, a steady stream of water poured from a spout, pooling in the tub below. Praising herself she grinned, slapping her hands together before yanking on the leather binding her breasts. In mere seconds, the material covering her body fell to the floor and she stepped into the tub, the coolness of the water refreshing as she shifted her legs into her iridescent turquoise tail.

Even though the water was colder than she would have liked, since she didn't know how to get hot water out of the spout, or if that was even possible, Ocevia leaned back, relaxation loosening her muscles. The tub was small and the end of Ocevia's tail draped over the end, but she was still able to use a glass beside the tub to pour water over the entirety of it. She knew she was making a mess, but as she sang a tune she made up as she went along, she didn't care. So caught up in singing and bathing, Ocevia hadn't noticed Azure enter her guest room until her friend called out to her.

"Ocevia? Food is ready."

Ocevia stopped singing, looking around to see that there was more water on the floor than she'd realized. "Hey! I'm in the tub."

Entering the bathing room a moment later, Azure snickered. "You're lucky it's only me and not one of the wait staff checking in on you."

Ocevia shrugged, lifting the glass of water to rinse her long blond locks. "Well, they shouldn't enter my room uninvited."

Rolling her eyes, Azure nodded toward the bedroom door. "It was unlocked."

"I haven't been in the human lands since I was a child. I couldn't figure out how to lock it. I don't know how to use half the stuff in here. It took me forever just to figure out how to turn the water on."

Azure's lips twisted, guilt flashing in her eyes. "I'm sorry, Ocevia. I should have shown you around and explained things to you."

Hoping to ease the guilt her friend had no reason to feel, Ocevia smirked, shifting back into her legs and pulling the drain at the bottom of the tub. "Don't worry about it. I'm the one who ran off at the promise of a tub. If you and your hunk of manliness give me food and clothes, I'm sure I can figure out how to use the bed on my own. I don't plan on doing much other than sleeping after I eat."

As Ocevia stepped out of the tub, reaching for a fluffy piece of white cloth to dry herself, Azure turned back toward the door. "I'll bring in a plate of food and a glass of wine for you while you dry off. I expect they'll bring up clothing soon. I'll be right back."

Sliding the soft cloth against her skin, Ocevia watched as her friend disappeared into the darkened room, the door hinges near silent as she opened the door and then closed it behind her.

Without clean clothes to wear, Ocevia sauntered back into the room with the bed, gooseflesh puckering her skin in the chilly air. Kneeling in front of the fireplace, she took some logs out of a basket against the wall. She stacked them, looking for the most suitable tender to spark a flame. The door reopened and Azure walked in with a tray of food in her hands. Her friend crossed the room quickly and reached above the mantle for a small metal object before kneeling beside her.

For the next several minutes, Azure taught Ocevia how to start a fire using a fire starter. She then walked her through the room, showing her the different amenities and how to use them. Ocevia was in awe of the gadgets and conveniences she could have only dreamed of when living in the sea. The herby aroma of their dinner lured her to the large bowl of stew just as a knock sounded at the door. Azure opened the door only a few inches, allowing Elios to slip a small bundle of clothing through the crack.

Helping her dress into a long white top that tied down the front and a loose pair of trousers, Azure left Ocevia alone in the silent room.

Picking up the plate of food and the glass of wine, Ocevia padded across the small room, settling in the chair in front of the window. She placed her meal on the sill and pulled off the clothing her friend had given her, the fabric rubbing against her skin in an uncomfortable way. It had been a decade since she'd worn human clothes. She knew she would have to get used to them, but for now, while she was alone in her room, she could let her skin breathe.

As Ocevia lowered herself into the wooden chair, gazing out at the starlit mountain range beyond the city, overwhelming emotions invaded her senses. Fear of being recaptured by Miris. Trepidation about venturing further into the unknown. Excitement at the possibility of living on land. Her heartbeats were heavy, the air in the room too thin.

Part of her wanted to run to Azure, needing something familiar to comfort her, but she couldn't do that. It was no longer just the two of them. Azure had Elios now, leaving Ocevia alone. A tear trailed down Ocevia's cheek, her loneliness palpable in the room. After a moment of allowing herself to process the emotion, she wiped the tear from her cheek and took a heaping bite of her stew.

Even though it was lukewarm, flavors burst across Ocevia's tongue, pulling a groan from her throat. She ate another spoonful of the concoction, barely chewing on the meat and vegetables before swallowing them down. When the spoon hit the bottom of the bowl, Ocevia lifted the glass of deep red liquid, taking a deep sip of it and nearly spitting it back out. She realized there was a reason people drank the stuff, but it was bitter on her tongue. Standing and returning to the bathing room, she poured the wine down the drain and filled the glass with water before returning to her spot in front of the window.

With a piece of fresh bread hanging out of her mouth, Ocevia lowered herself back into the chair. She opened the window a crack, inhaling deeply as the sea breeze fluttered through the sheer curtains. She closed her eyes, smiling as the satisfaction of a full belly and the comfort of her surroundings filled her with a sense of safety for the first time in her life.

CHAPTER 13

THE CIRCLE

L ight streamed through the open window, a cool
breeze skating across Ocevia's bare skin and pulling
her from a deep sleep. She'd sat in front of the window
for hours, anticipation replacing her earlier exhaustion.

When her eyelids had become too heavy to keep up, she'd
moved to the bed, moaning as the soft bedding embraced
her naked body as though she were floating in the clouds.

She'd drifted off to sleep as soon as her head had settled
on the pillow.

Rolling over in the blanket, it took her a moment to
remember where she was. A bright smile spread across
her lips as the sound of birds filled her ears. She sprung

out of bed, racing toward the door to find her friend. The moment her hand grabbed the handle, however, she let it go and returned to the pile of clothing on the floor. She looked at it for a moment, huffing out a groan as she bent over to scoop it up. After living for so long without clothing, the garments made little sense to her. However, she tugged the large white top over her head, not bothering with the straps before tugging the trousers up her legs. With not even a glance in the looking glass, Ocevia darted across the hall and banged on her friend's door.

Although she could hear footsteps inside the room beyond the door, and hear muffled voices, it took Azure and Elios a moment to answer. Ocevia's grin grew, intending to ask her friend what bedding a male was like when they had time alone. She didn't know for sure if Azure and Elios had gotten that far, but by how they were together, she had little doubt they had. As she fumbled with the straps on her tunic, heavy footsteps approached, and the door swung open.

With his hair disheveled and his clothes as haphazardly pulled on as Ocevia's, any doubt that her friend was still innocent was put to rest. Behind her lover, Azure fastened the laces of her own tunic, but her eyes widened as Ocevia met her eyes. Before Ocevia could greet her, Azure darted across the room, grabbing her by the arm and pulling her inside.

"Ocevia." Exasperation filled Azure's voice as she reached for the ties on Ocevia's top, pulling them tight before tying them. Ocevia tried to watch the movement, so she could repeat it in the future, but her friend's hands moved too quickly. "You can't stand in the hallway half-dressed."

Taken aback, Ocevia looked down at her clothing, incredulity on her face when she returned her eyes to her friend. "I usually wear way less than this, Azure. You're being ridiculous."

Clearly holding back, Azure braced her hands on Ocevia's shoulders. "Mermaids wear less, but humans don't. Remember, you're pretending to be human right now."

With how unfamiliar she was with human customs, Ocevia didn't argue, and Azure seemed relieved. "So, what's the plan for today?" Azure asked, eyeing them both as she waited for a response.

Sitting on the bed, Elios laced up his boots quickly. Ocevia watched him in amazement. She hoped to learn how to do that one day. "Let's head down to the tavern for breakfast first." When he turned his eyes up to Azure for confirmation, her cheeks reddened with a flush that had Ocevia stifling a snicker.

"Or I can have it brought up, if you'd prefer," he added.

Excited to mingle with the other humans, and unwilling to eat another meal alone, Ocevia turned and darted toward the door, hoping her friends would follow.

Just as was the case the night before, the tavern was filled with people, all chatting and enjoying their breakfast. Their smiles brought one to Ocevia's face as well.

Following Elios and Azure, Ocevia sat down at a table in the corner and Elios ordered three daily breakfast specials. After how delicious her dinner had been the night before, Ocevia's stomach was already grumbling and ready to be filled with more.

As they waited for their meal to arrive, she couldn't help but scan the space, taking in the faces of the patrons, admiring their clothes, shoes, and the way they spoke to each other. So much about her world had changed since she'd left it, and she had never lived in Starspell. Her home, which was in Thatia, was on the other side of the Lamalis sea. Life was different there, especially for a child who was unable to go to these types of establishments that she could now visit as an adult.

Knowing she longed for romance, Ocevia studied the faces of every male who looked close enough to her age, but to her disappointment, none of them filled her with the spark that told her he could be her mate.

The approaching server, and the smell of food pulled Ocevia's attention away from the crowd and back to her friends and the meal laid out before her. Although she'd had eggs and fried potatoes before, it had been so long ago that she couldn't imagine the taste. Her memories of food prior to her life in the sea were too few and faded.

The moment the eating utensil was in her hand, Ocevia dug it into her breakfast, scooping an extra-large serving into her mouth and groaning as her eyes rolled back in her head with how delicious it was. "This is so good." Her words were a mixture of speech and a moan as she swallowed her food down and took a sip of her tea. Before it had even cleared her throat, she shoveled more food into her mouth, groaning once more.

Ocevia was so enthralled by her breakfast, nearly ready to bring it to her bed, that she didn't even notice if her friends were eating at all. If they had been eating, they'd certainly not been as dramatic as she had, but she didn't care. She'd never been one to get embarrassed easily. After a decade of eating mostly raw or dried fish, any home cooked meal was like ecstasy in her mouth. When her utensil scraped against the empty plate and her stomach made a strange noise, Ocevia finally looked up at her friends. Azure and Elios sat across from her with empty plates as well, but they both stared at her as though she was a feral animal.

Before she had a chance to ask them why they were looking at her like that, a middle-aged female came to the table and dropped off several bags of clothing and supplies. According to Elios, the female was the bar owner's wife.

Ocevia was excited to dig inside the bags and see what types of human items they'd been given, but before she could, Vasso approached their table from across the bar, and took Elios by the wrist, catching him by surprise. With an unspoken understanding on their faces, Elios rose from the table and allowed the older male to lead him into the darkened hallway near the stairwell. Ocevia's stomach sank with unease, but she stood as well, and with Azure by her side, she followed the males.

It was clear from Vasso's face that whatever he had to tell them was important, but the way his eyes shifted from side to side, as though he was searching for something, also made it clear that whatever he had to tell them was a secret. His behavior only made the sinking feeling in Ocevia's stomach worsen.

Just when Ocevia was about to ask him what was going on, Vasso leaned in close to them, speaking in no more than a whisper.

"I don't mean to rush you off, Elios, but there were some individuals digging around in town late last night, looking for a woman with her description." The way he turned his gaze to her friend brought burning dread into Ocevia's throat. Someone was looking for them, and that someone could only be those sent by Miris. Swallowing thickly, Ocevia reached out and slid her hand into Azure's. Fear paled Azure's face, but she remained silent. "They came into the tavern after the three of you went to bed. I didn't recognize either of them under their heavy cloaks, but I ran their asses off. I doubt they've left the city, though. It's not safe for you here."

CHAPTER 14

THE DARK-HAIRED MALE

Seeming resigned, but unsurprised, Elios rubbed his eyebrows as he thought for a moment before speaking. "Send word to our contacts. We'll set out for Ceveasea today."

Vasso took another glance toward Elios and his female companions, dipping his chin in acknowledgement. "I can spare a few men from The Circle. I don't want you leaving with these ladies without a few extra swords."

With a sharp nod, Elios reached for Azure's hand and urged her and Ocevia back up the stairs. A muscle in his jaw ticked as they walked, showing the tension he was trying to hide.

Ocevia didn't know what "The Circle" was, but it sounded important, and like something Elios was deeply involved in. She wanted to know more, *needed* to know more, but as quickly as Elios moved down the hall, leading them in a rush to get out of the city, she knew it wasn't the right time to ask questions.

Remaining silent as they walked down the hall, Elios opened the door to their room, and then led Ocevia and Azure inside. "Take a moment to wet your tails while you can. I'll get our packs together. I know you understood what Vasso said. They're already here looking for us. If we don't get out of the city now, we may never be able to leave."

The bile in Ocevia's throat rose, sending a disgusting taste into her mouth that she tried to swallow back down.

She turned to walk toward the bathing room, needing to do something, anything, but stopped when Azure didn't follow her. "Elios," Azure said, hesitation in her voice. "What's The Circle?"

Reaching forward, Elios took Azure's hand in his, immense stress showing on his face. His eyes scanned the room once before turning his eyes back to look at her. "I promise to tell you everything once we're safe. But for now, we need to get moving. I'd imagine Vasso is preparing the horses and men now. The sooner we leave, the better. The longer we wait, the more danger you'll be in, we'll all be in."

Ocevia knew it wasn't the answer she and her best friend deserved, but she also realized that Elios was right.

If Miris' henchmen were already in the city, they needed to leave immediately. The Sea Goddess had a very far reach, so if they had any chance of escaping her, they had to stay many steps ahead of her.

Grabbing clean trousers and boots out of the new bag, Azure handed a set to Ocevia and then rushed into her own bathing room to do as they were instructed. With only a moment of hesitation, Ocevia left the safety of her friends' room and returned across the hall into her own, intending to soak her tail quickly. She didn't want to be away from them any longer than she had to be.

When they returned downstairs and out the back door of the tavern only moments later, several satchels lay on the ground, stuffed to the brim with supplies for them to take on their journey. Several men stood near four horses, along with Vasso and his wife, Chryssa.

As the barkeep's wife approached them and handed Elios another bag that was filled with water skins and food, one of the males in the clearing caught Ocevia's attention. Although she didn't know his name, the pull from him on her heart was like magic.

As the rest of the world went on around her, as their group readied to leave Starspell, she couldn't look away from him. Standing next to an onyx horse, his shoulder-length hair the same color, the male chewed on a piece of straw, paying very little attention to them, or to her. With her heart thundering in her chest, Ocevia silently begged him to look up at her, but he didn't seem to hear her silent pleas.

One of the males, tall and muscular like Elios but with bright red hair and a full beard to match, approached them with a smile on his face that challenged the sun's brightness. Ocevia reluctantly looked away from the male near the trees, as the redhead greeted them and wrapped his arms around Elios' shoulder.

It became clear to Ocevia quickly that Dimitris Teresides' personality was as bright as his hair, and she couldn't help but to giggle at the enthusiasm in everything he said.

While the horses were being saddled, Dimitris and Elios talked as though they were old friends just catching up. She didn't know much about either male, but it was clear that's exactly what they were. *Friends.*

When it got closer to the time for them to leave, once the horses were saddled and their belongings tucked safely in the saddle bags, nervousness moved in, causing Ocevia to shift from foot to foot. She'd never ridden on a horse before, and didn't know enough about them to know if it was safe.

Seeming to notice her unease, Azure moved to her side and grasped Ocevia's hand. "Are you okay?"

"I don't know how to ride a horse, Azure. That thing may kill me." Ocevia never turned her stare away from the horses as she answered her friend's question.

Shrugging, Azure squeezed her hand gently. "I haven't ridden a horse since I was younger, and have barely any experience either, but I'm sure you won't be by yourself. You'll ride with one of those fine men." Although Azure flourished her hand, indicating that Ocevia could ride with any of the males in their group, there was only one she intended to ride with, even if he still hadn't turned up to look at her. She had, however, learned his name. Listening in to Dimitris and Elios catch up, she learned that the male she was attracted to was named Markos.

The fourth male, the tallest and approximately a decade older than the others, was named Aris. Even without knowing anything about Aris, Ocevia could tell that he had lived an adventurous life. His arms were covered in tattoos, and he had long, golden hair that was tied back in a strap. Not only was he taller than the other three males but he was also incredibly muscular, toned with broad shoulders, as though he had been fighting with weapons his entire life. Still, even with the long hair and the countless tattoos, his honey brown eyes and his smile were warm, disarming Ocevia a little. At least in his face, he appeared to be kind. Neither Aris nor Markos had spoken much at all as they all congregated behind the tavern. It seemed as though Dimitris spoke enough for the three of them.

As their conversation shifted to readying to leave, Ocevia turned her glance back to the male she wanted, only to catch him gazing back at her, his bright green eyes like summer grass. For a moment, she was unable to speak, frozen in place, until Azure squeezed her hand.

"I want that one, I think." Shamelessly lifting her hand in front of her, Ocevia pointed right at Markos, the unabashed gesture making Azure laugh.

Her snickers silencing, her friend patted her on the back.

"I'm not sure if you get to choose, but I'll see what I can do." As Azure walked away to speak to Elios, Ocevia remained where she stood, keeping her eyes on Markos as he turned to pet his horse, flicking his eyes back at her a few times.

CHAPTER 15

MARKOS

Interrupting Ocevia and Markos' awkward moment, Elios called out, "Hey, Markos."

Markos' body jerked as Elios' voice seemed to catch him by surprise. Turning away from Ocevia, he turned and jogged toward Elios. Ocevia couldn't hear what they were saying, but she didn't miss Elios' mischievous grin, which sent a flush to her own cheeks. A moment later, Markos nodded, and then he turned and began walking toward Ocevia. Her heart flipped, but her body stiffened as he closed the distance between them. She'd never been a shy person, but the closer he got, the more speechless she became.

"Ocevia?" he asked, holding out his hand in front of him.

The warm flush that crept up Ocevia's cheeks burned hotter as she nodded and held her hand out to let him take it. The side of his mouth tipped up in a small grin, and it nearly brought her to her knees.

"Elios said you would like to ride with me?"

Although it had been a statement, he'd framed it as a question, just in case she changed her mind. Ocevia nodded again, still too shy to speak.

Lifting her hand to his mouth, he kissed her knuckles, holding her gaze for a moment before setting her hand back down. "Well, it's nice to meet you, Ocevia. My name is Markos. My steed's name is Storm. Can I walk you to him and help you onto the saddle?"

The kind way he spoke to her broke the spell he'd held over her just enough so she could speak.

"Yes, but I have a confession." Her voice was so low that he leaned in to hear her better, sending his scent into her nose and making her heart flutter.

"And what is your confession, Ocevia?"

She thought about telling him that she was in love with him, that she wanted to marry him and have all his babies but decided against it. "I've never ridden a horse, and I am a bit terrified."

Grinning, he slid his hand to the small of her back and led her toward his horse as the rest of their group mounted their saddles.

The first thing she realized when she got close enough to see the pupils of its black eyes, was that the horse was so much bigger up close than she'd realized. Trying to calm her, Markos threaded his fingers in hers, and then lifted their joined hands to the horse's side, smoothing its black fur.

"Storm may look intimidating, but he's kind as long as you're kind to him. Neither him, nor I, will let anything bad happen to you. You have my word."

The genuine look in his green eyes was hypnotizing, their stair only broke when he slipped his hands around her waist and lifted her. He set her on the saddle as though she weighed no more than an infant. A moment later, he mounted the horse behind her, pulling her flush against his chest as she sat between his thighs. With his powerful arms wrapped around her sides, he grabbed the reins.

Warmth spread through her body at his closeness, pooling between her legs. It was a sensation like she had never felt before. Desire. Although she had never been close to a male, had never been touched by a male, there was no doubt in her mind that the sensation Markos gave her by being close to her, was desire, lust.

She readjusted her hips on the saddle, needing friction against the sensitive spot between her thighs. She'd never been touched by a male before, but she'd touched herself enough to know that it felt good. If she got her way, then Markos would touch her soon. As they set off along the back alleys of Starspell and toward the mountain range, it was all Ocevia could think about. She needed Markos to touch her—to kiss her—to bed her—to do everything with her that she'd never been able to do before but was ready to do now.

Since they traveled down the back alleys of the city, there weren't many people there to recognize them. Still, the entire group wore hooded black cloaks just in case. Ocevia did not believe the rest of the group knew that she and Azure were mermaids, but they did seem to know that the two females in their company were in danger and needed to be escorted out of the city in secrecy. With that thought, Ocevia also realized that she would need to tell Markos about her true nature eventually, especially if she wanted him to take her to his bed. She did not want to tell him about the monster hiding in her necklace, however. That was something she wanted no one to know. All he needed to know about was her tail.

As they moved out of the city, the cobblestone streets turned into a dirt path that brought them out of the alleys, and toward the pass between the mountains. The horses' steps clacked as they hit the ground, making a cadence that threatened to put Ocevia to sleep. Markos' arms were still wrapped tightly around her as his hands controlled the reins of the horse. For much of the ride, Ocevia allowed her eyes to close as his strong body warmed her, imagining what it would be like if it was their skin touching and not their clothing.

Once they moved into the mountain pass, it seemed they no longer needed to be quiet to avoid unwanted attention. Muffled voices met Ocevia's ears as Azure and Elios held a muffled conversation just ahead of them, Elios holding her friend tightly as they rode. Aris led the way, while Dimitris held up the rear of their group, trailing just behind her and Markos.

Reaching forward to rub her hand across the horse's soft mane, Ocevia licked her lips. "Do you have a wife, Markos?"

Seeming to not expect the Ocevia's question, Markos huffed out to laugh. "Well, that was an unexpected question, Ocevia. No... I do not have a wife. Do you have a husband?"

She hadn't expected him to respond to her inquiry about his personal life, so when he did, she couldn't help but grin - not just at his answer, but at the fact that he had given one at all. "Where I'm from, having a lover is not allowed. I don't really get a chance to interact with human men." A tinge of guilt hit her chest, knowing she'd killed thousands of people. She'd interacted with them, just not in the way he was thinking. Although she realized he would eventually learn the truth about her, she swallowed back the burn of guilt and blew out a breath. "I've never had a lover, or even been kissed...I want to though."

As the words rolled off her tongue, his body seemed to stiffen around her. "You don't get the opportunity to go on dates? To get married?"

Confusion had Ocevia's eyebrows creasing, and she turned over her shoulder to look at him. "What's a date?"

In the most handsome of gestures, his eyebrow lifted, arching in the middle. "Why my lovely, Ocevia, it seems you have missed out on a lot. Maybe, once we get somewhere safe, and if you would like, I could take you on your first date. But to answer your question, a date is when a man takes a woman somewhere nice so he can woo her and make her fall in love with him."

Before the words had finished leaving his lips, she was already nodding. "Yes! I would love for you to woo me...but I think I'm already in love with you."

The chuckle that left Markos' lips had Ocevia curling in on herself with embarrassment. She wondered if she'd said something wrong, but if she had, she didn't know what it was.

Markos, realizing he had hurt her feelings, let go of the reins with one hand, sliding it down her arm to interlace his fingers with hers. "My apologies if I hurt your feelings, little one. I didn't mean to do that. It's just that... I've never had a woman tell me they love me the moment they met me."

Turning around to face him, she smirked. "That's a good thing, since you're supposed to be my mate, not theirs."

Markos smiled back at her, lifting his finger to trace along her jawbone. Her eyes fell closed, his touch sending shivers racing down her spine. "Your mate, huh? Is that what I am supposed to be to you?"

With a slow nod, she leaned into his hand as he cupped her cheek. "My heart says so."

As her eyes lay closed, enjoying the feel of his calloused hand against her face, warm lips touched her cheek in a gentle kiss. "Your heart can't lie to you, so it must be right. Maybe later, you'll let me kiss you again, and you can tell me more about being your mate."

Shivers continue to race down her body, gooseflesh puckering along her arms and legs as the area between her thighs throbbed with the need. "You could kiss me now."

His eyebrow lifting into a point again, Markos grinned at her before taking in their surroundings, something flashing across his eyes that she couldn't decipher.

"If you really want me to kiss you, little one, then I promise I will when we get somewhere safe. But, at least for now, we need to speed up our pace and find shelter for the night. It's not safe to be out in the open in these mountains past nightfall. Things come out in the darkness that we don't want to cross paths with."

As she turned back to look in front of them, a slight tinge of disappointment in her chest, coupled with fear from Markos' ominous warning, he dug his heels into the horse's sides, urging Storm to go faster. A beat later, they were riding right next to Elios and Azure.

"Any ideas where you want to stop tonight, Brother?" Markos asked Elios with his arms still wrapped snugly around Ocevia's waist. Azure was tucked in close to Elios as well, with her cloak wrapped firmly around her. Knowing Markos intended to kiss her, and seeing her friend happy with her own lover, sent Ocevia's heart soaring.

Before responding, Elios glanced up to scan the sky, as though he were looking for something. "We need a place we can defend, somewhere with a water source, before sundown. You know the creatures that roam these lands at night. I don't want to be vulnerable once we lose the protection of daylight."

Their words sent burning fear into Ocevia's chest, but she tried not to let it overcome her because Markos had promised that he would keep her safe. He twisted to look at Dimitris before responding to Elios again. "There's a camp about five hours from here. Maybe less if we pick up the pace."

"Let's try to get there before sundown."

Without another word, Markos followed Elios' order, digging his heels into the Storm's side again. They galloped forward toward where they would stay for the night as Ocevia watched the sky, hoping the sun would wait until they arrived to take its slumber.

CHAPTER 16

LITTLE SEA MAIDEN

After a long ride at a heavy gallop, the group reached the place where they would spend the night just before sundown. Ocevia still wanted to know what types of creatures lived in those mountains at night, but they had been moving at too quick of a pace for her and Markos to have a conversation. A chill ran through her as they rode, looking out at the cliffs and wondering what kind of beast could frighten the four large men and their friends.

From a distance, Ocevia would have never known the extent of the village very deep within the mountain pass. From the main road, it only looked like winding canyons and cliffs scattered with caves of various sizes. Once they got close, however, she realized that the settlement was quite large, with dozens of men, women, and children, all living in the caves that lined the base of the mountain range. I Storms, loaded steps, Ocevia gates, around at the community, noticing the large bonfire in the center, where the scent of roasted meat walked her through the air, making her hungry. They ate snacks along the way, but nothing substantial enough to fill her belly as much as the human food had at the tavern.

Moving ahead of their group, Markos squeezed Ocevia's hand, before dismounting from the horse and handing the reins to Dimitris as Ocevia remained on the saddle. She watched as he walked away from their group and toward a large male carrying a spear. It was clear by the male's appearance that he rarely, if ever, visited modern society. His black hair was in long braids that reached past his backside, large feathers shooting out of the top of the braid, and the spear in his hand was primitive, not like the weapons Elios and the other men in her group carried.

The group waited for a moment, not moving forward as Markos spoke to the male in private. When Markos walked back toward them, the spear-carrying man by his side, a smile lifting the side of his mouth, easing a bit of the tension that had built up in Ocevia's body while waiting.

If this tribe refused to allow them to stay, they would be forced to retreat back out into the pass where the monsters were. Thinking about the creatures in the mountains only reminded Ocevia of the monster hiding inside her necklace. A chill ran through her blood and she squeezed the cool shell in her hand, pushing the thoughts away.

"We can stay," Markos said, lifting his hand toward the male at his side. "This is a tribal elder, Great Protector." The large man nodded once and walked away without a word. "Great Protector said we can take the caves at the far end." Markos pointed to the right side of the cliffs. "There are a few rooms inside and water for drinking and bathing. He exchanged gold for the night."

As Elios nodded, motioning for their group to follow him, Markos mounted Storm again, sliding in just behind Ocevia, and kissing her on the cheek. She shivered, the light touch sending warmth through her.

"Are you tired, my little sea maiden?" Markos asked, his lips close enough to send his breath skittering across her cheek. The desire that filled her from his closeness nearly made her miss what he'd called her.

Twisting on the saddle, she looked into his green eyes, searching for something in them, although she wasn't sure what. "Why did you call me a sea maiden?"

He was quiet for a moment as his eyes scanned the camp around them, seeming to make sure no one was listening. "Great Protector told me that you and your friend were mermaids. I didn't want to believe him, but he insisted. He said you were in great danger, and that the Sea Goddess would be looking to reclaim you. Is that why we're hiding you, Ocevia? Did she enslave you?"

For the second time that day, Ocevia was speechless. If she told him the truth, would he turn her over? Sure, she was drawn to him, but that didn't mean he was a good man, it didn't mean he would protect her against a goddess, especially if that goddess was offering a hefty reward. Ignoring the question for a moment, Ocevia spun around in the saddle, putting her back to Markos once more.

As her heart thundered against her rib cage, almost painfully, her mind fumbled with what to do. Part of her wanted to jump off the horse, grab her friend, and run.

They'd already come too far to be recaptured and dragged back to Miris' dungeons. Seeming to sense her fear and her hesitation, Markos slid his hand around her waist and pulled her closer to him so he could speak directly into her ear.

"Do not be afraid of me, Ocevia. Whether you're a mermaid running from the Sea Goddess, or a human slave running from a master, I will protect you with my life."

Some of the tightness in her chest eased with his words, and she hoped they were genuine. "If we get caught, we—"

Her words were cut off as Markos tucked the hair behind her ear and interrupted her. "I'm not going to let you get caught. I give you my word that I will give my life to protect you."

Leaning into his touch, she nodded. "And Great Protector? Will he turn us in?"

Markos shook his head. "The Arcane River Tribe do not associate with civilization much. They sustain themselves on a simpler way of life. He assured me that no one else would know. He also told me that there's a hot spring that runs along the back of the cave system. He said it's perfect for you and Azure to wet your tails if you need to."

As Ocevia pondered Markos' words, they approached one of the larger caves, its opening closed off with a wooden gate. Storm's steps slowed as a tribal member approached them, lifting his hand to take the reins from

Markos. Peering inside, Ocevia noticed that the large cave closed with a gate was a stable, meant to protect their livestock from any predators in the mountains. She only hoped the place they would spend the night would have such protection.

As soon as the reins were in the young tribal males' hands, Markos dismounted before reaching up and grabbing Ocevia by the waist, lifting her off the horse and setting her down in front of him. For a moment, their gazes locked, neither of them looking away for several beats of Ocevia's heart.

In her peripheral vision, Ocevia noticed Elios place Azure on the ground. As Azure leaned over to stretch her limbs and back, she shot Ocevia a smile.

Elios called out to Markos, so Ocevia left his side and approached her friend. There were certainly a lot of things they needed to discuss.

"Markos said there is a heated river inside!" The words practically bubbled out of Ocevia's mouth, making her friend's smile widen.

"Are you having fun? You seem awfully happy."

A flush coming to her cheeks, Ocevia patted Azure on the arm. "Yes. I am, actually. Markos smells so good, and he's been such a gentleman. Plus, he's *really* handsome."

Azure reached for Ocevia's hand as they followed behind the males toward the cave entrance. "Well, I'm glad you've enjoyed his company since you were stuck on a horse with him all day. Do you still want to ride with him tomorrow?"

Excited to spend more time with Markos, Ocevia picked up her pace. "Of course, I'm going to ride with him again. I'm *going* to make him my husband."

Although the look on Azure's face told Ocevia that her friend didn't necessarily reach her enthusiasm, she'd meant every word. Markos would be hers and she would be his. It was the one thing in the world she was sure about.

When they arrived in the large cavernous space that would be their home for the night, Azure squeezed Ocevia's hand as she turned to face her.

"You don't have to tell him about... us... if you're not ready. You can always wait until he sleeps to soak *properly*. Don't feel pressured."

With a warm embrace, Azure turned and walked away. Ocevia opened her mouth to call out to her, to tell her about the conversation she and Markos had just had but closed it again. Markos already knew she was a mermaid, but it would have to remain their secret for now.

CHAPTER 17

DARE TO DREAM

The cluster of caves where they would sleep was larger than Ocevia had anticipated. Each doorway led to the sleeping quarters, with a leather screen blocking each entrance. There was a fireplace in the main room and a fire was already burning inside. The sulfuric smell of the hot spring filled her nose. In the back of their cavern, there was a large pool fed by a stream that snaked through their cavern, leading to both of their neighbors.

As Azure walked away from Ocevia, heading toward an opening on the right side of the main chamber, Markos waited for Ocevia with his hand outstretched. It seemed she wasn't the only one who realized Azure and Elios would want privacy. Since her friend now had a lover who she would continue to pair off with, the rest of their group had to decide where everyone else would sleep in the multiroom cave system.

"If you'd like to take a room by yourself, I can set myself up in the main room," Markos said as he led her behind one of the leather screens and into a small room set up like a bed chamber. A platform against one of the walls was covered with blankets made of animal fur, but aside from a small fire pit near the center where the ceiling was the highest, the rest of the space was bare. Crossing the room, Ocevia lowered herself onto the platform, running her hands across the silky animal fur. It was like nothing she'd ever felt before.

"I don't want to sleep alone." Sliding over a few inches, she patted the bed beside her. "There's enough space for both of us on the bed."

Markos watched her for a moment, his eyebrow lifting as he unbuckled his weapon belt and dropped it to the floor. "How about I stay in the room with you, but I can make a bed on the floor. I'll still be close, little one."

Pulse quickening, desperate for him to touch her, Ocevia crossed her arms over her chest, rubbing them to warm them. "It's so cold in here. Much too cold for you to sleep on the floor."

With the side of his lip going in the way of his eyebrow, Markos kneeled next to the firepit, using the flint to get the fire started. Ocevia watched him, her lips twisting as she debated her next excuse for him to sleep with her. Wearing a thick cloak on top of her tunic and trousers, she wasn't really cold, and she was pretty sure Markos knew that. She was manipulating him. They both knew it, but she didn't care. At any moment, Miris' scouts could find her and drag her back to the dungeon to be beaten and murdered. While she had the chance to experience life like a real woman, like a free woman, she intended to take it.

As the fire caught and the blaze grew larger, creating more light in the dark space, Markos stood back up and sat on the bed beside her. He blew out a breath, remaining silent for several violent beats of her heart. When he finally turned to look at her, the fire flickering off his green eyes, his hand slid into hers, interlacing their fingers. Her breath caught, anticipation making it difficult to breathe.

"I can't imagine what you've been through, Ocevia, or what it's taken for you to get here." He paused, rubbing the top of her hand with his thumb. "It's clear there is something between us, but I do not want to rush it."

Even though he wasn't denying her feelings, the words still sent her heart plummeting to her stomach. He must have noticed the shift in her emotions, because his other hand slid up to cup her face, tilting her face back up to look at his. "Please do not take my words as me turning you down, little one. That is so far from what I'm saying. All I'm saying is that I don't ever want you to feel like I took advantage of your vulnerability. We may not know each other well yet, but I know you're special. I want real love to grow between us before you give your body to me."

Although she knew he meant what he said, tears still burned the back of her eyes, one finding its way down her cheek. The moment he noticed it; guilt flashed across his face as he swiped it away with his thumb. Wrapping his arm around her back, he pulled her closer against his side, kissing her on the top of her head. "Talk to me, my sea maiden. I never meant to make you cry. Tell me how to make it better."

She shrugged as the words lingered on her tongue, too scared to say them out loud. "I don't know how much time I have left."

The moment the words left her lips, she knew they were true, and she could no longer stop the tears that had been lingering just behind her eyes. Markos pulled her onto his lap, wrapping her in a tight embrace as he pressed his lips to the side of her face. Even with the pain in her chest, his closeness filled her with need.

"Don't talk like that, Ocevia. Don't think like that. We'll leave here tomorrow and keep moving inland until the Sea Goddess is too far away to ever find you. I'm not going to let her take you back there. I promise you."

She nodded against his chest, his heartbeat calming in her ear. "I know the four of you will do whatever you can to help Azure and I escape, but you don't know Miris. Her reach is farther than even I know. She could be watching this camp right now and we wouldn't know. I never dared to dream about having a mate, about finding love. It was something I knew would never be possible for me, but see-ing Azure with Elios... and then meeting you... It's just—"

Warm lips brushed against Ocevia's, cutting off her ad-mission. The touch was tentative at first, but when she didn't pull away, Markos slid his fingers into her hair, slanting his lips over hers and kissing her harder. Ocevia melted against him, her body responding to his touch as if it had been waiting for it her entire life.

In all her twenty-one years of life, Ocevia had never experienced something so divine as Markos' pillow-soft lips pressed against hers as his intoxicating scent filled her senses. He groaned against her mouth, parting her lips with his tongue to taste her. Although she didn't know if she kissed him correctly, he didn't seem to mind. She opened for him, daring to slide her tongue against his as her arms wrapped around his neck, twisting them in his dark hair.

Time stood still as their lips explored one another, the rest of the world falling away around them. When he pulled away, he leaned his forehead against hers as they tried to catch their breaths.

She wanted to kiss him again, wanted anything he would give her. However, a head of red hair peeked in through the cave's makeshift door before they could move any further. "There's roasted meat outside if you two are hungry."

CHAPTER 18

THE ARCANE RIVER TRIBE

Although Dimitris had ducked out of the doorway as soon as he saw Ocevia and Markos in each other's arms, the moment had passed. With everyone outside eating, their absence would surely draw too much attention. With everything being so new, the last thing they wanted to do was answer questions about their budding relationship. Ocevia hoped, however, that things would progress once everyone went to sleep that night.

Leaving the privacy of their cave behind, Ocevia and Markos headed back out into the late-night air toward the largest bonfire in the valley. To her delight, he held her hand as they walked, the touch filling her with a sense of safety, even if it was only surface deep.

As they moved closer to where dozens of tribal people were gathered, along with Aris and Dimitris, the aroma of roasted meat wafted along the breeze, reminding her of just how hungry she was. An enormous animal carcass hung over the flames on a long wooden spit, although Ocevia was not sure of the species. She didn't have to wonder for long, however, since Dimitris ran up to them, holding out a heaping plate of meat and saying, "You have got to taste this roasted bear! Here! Taste this," he said, lifting a greasy chunk of meat off the plate and holding it toward Ocevia's mouth. She giggled and shuffled back.

Markos chuckled, wrapping his arm around Ocevia's waist and pulling her close. "We'll get some in a bit, Brother. What I am curious about is what you've been drinking that has you frolicking around the camp trying to shove greasy meat into people's mouths."

Dimitris' eyes, which were already glazed over from drinking alcohol, widened. Although Ocevia didn't know much about drinking alcoholic beverages, she was surprised it had affected the large man so quickly. "Special brew the Arcane tribe makes themselves." Pivoting where he stood, their friend began walking back in the other direction. "Follow me, Brother. I'll get a mug of it for you."

When Dimitris was several yards ahead of them, Markos turned to look down at her, a smirk on his face. "My friend tends to drink whiskey as efficiently as a fish drinks water. Feel free to smack him away the next time he tries to stick a hunk of greasy meat in your face."

The expression on Markos' face, coupled with his words, sprung a giggle from Ocevia. "I'll definitely keep that in mind. However, the meat does smell amazing, and I am starving. I've never had bear before though."

Pulling her bottom lip between her teeth, she watched as their hosts carved into the meat, several working together to make the process more efficient. Even in the late hour, people of all ages were present in the area around the main fire, children playing with toys as adults either worked on tasks or sat on logs and stone structures, carrying on conversations over plates of meat and mugs that appeared to be made of bone. Among those seated near the fire were Aris and Dimitris, but she didn't see Azure or Elios.

"Would you like to get something to eat and sit with the others?" Ocevia nodded as Markos slid his hand across the small of her back, gently nudging her toward the fire.

"I don't see Azure or Elios anywhere." Scanning the space between the cliffs and caverns again, the deep shadows surrounding them filled Ocevia with unease, but Markos' gentle strokes to her back worked to ease it.

"Everyone is tired. The last I saw them; they were going into one of the bedchambers. Maybe they're sleeping, or maybe they're doing something even more fun. Either way, I'm sure they'll join us eventually."

Ocevia knew he was right, and, if anything, she wished she and Markos were still in the private bedchamber themselves. No matter how strong his arms felt around her, how much safety they provided, she still couldn't help but to feel like her time of pretending to be a human woman was running out. Before it did, she wanted him to show her what it was like to have a lover, to indulge herself in pleasures of the flesh that she'd never experienced. Putting thoughts of later aside, Ocevia reached out and took the mug of clear liquid Dimitris thrusted into her hand, taking a deep sip and then spitting it onto the ground before it had even fully hit her tongue. "What are you trying to do to me?"

Horror spread across Dimitris' eyes as he worked to balance himself on two legs. Whatever was in that mug was strong enough to have him off-kilter. "Oh—I'm sorry, Miss. Perhaps the Arcane brew is too strong."

Ocevia placed the mug in Markos' hand as a grin spread across her cheeks, the gesture allowing Dimitris' posture to relax. As the slightly intoxicated man wandered away, Markos led Ocevia to where Aris was seated on a giant log among the tribe members, seeming to be telling a story that had the other eight people fully engaged.

One of the females, with a leather cloak wrapped around her and long black hair braided down her back, moved aside as they approached, allowing Markos and Ocevia to sit beside their friend. When Ocevia looked back in the direction Dimitris had wandered off to, she smiled, her heart warmed from the inside out at seeing Azure and Elios approaching them, the red-haired man wrapping them both in an overexaggerated hug.

"You guys have to try this drink the Arcane people brewed. Stronger than any whiskey I've ever had."

Dimitris was loud, clearly intoxicated, but Elios simply took the bone mug from his friend and patted him on the shoulder.

"You need to slow down, Brother, or you'll retch right off your horse come morning."

Just like Markos, Elios seemed to be well-versed in how to handle Dimitris when he'd had a little too much to drink. It was clear the males in their group had history together, and were good friends, so when Elios redirected his intoxicated friend, Dimitris didn't argue. Instead, he nodded, mumbling that he was going to get more food, and then wandered away.

Dropping onto the log next to Markos, Elios pulled Azure onto his lap, both sipping on the same bone mug of alcohol as they listened in to Aris' tale of the high seas.

They spent hours among the Arcane people, eating and drinking, enjoying the warm hospitality of the tribe who lived so far removed from modern society. As Ocevia sat next to Markos with his arm around her, giving her affectionate cuddles and kisses, she couldn't help but to see the allure of living in such an unencumbered way. After so many years of living in the sea, without a warm bed or even clothing, she didn't need big cities and modern conveniences to survive. All she needed was Markos by her side. With him, she knew she could be happy.

After a long day of travel, the group made their way back to the caves where they would spend the night, Ocevia's legs as heavy as her eyelids. Although she'd hoped to go to the hot spring with Markos, so she could show him who she really was and hope he found her mermaid form appealing, Azure reached for her as they entered the main space of the cavern.

"Elios will stand guard out here while we bathe. Would that be okay?"

With Azure still not knowing that Markos knew the truth, Ocevia nodded and followed her friend toward the pool in the deepest part of the cave system, looking over her shoulder as Markos took up a spot next to Elios at the bathing room's entrance.

CHAPTER 19
WHY WAIT?

As Ocevia and Azure left the area where the hot spring ran through the back of the caves, Markos stood beside Elios, a sleepy grin on his face. Her heart flipped at the sight of him, excitement of spending the night with him for the first time filling her. She realized he meant what he said, and that he wouldn't rush with her even if she wanted him to, but just being intimate with him at all was worth looking forward to.

Azure and Elios walked away, leaving the two of them alone near the main fire together. It was then that she realized his hair was damp, telling her he must have cleaned up in a separate part of the caverns while she and Azure were soaking.

"Are you ready to go to sleep, Ocevia?" Holding out his hand, Markos slipped it into hers, pulling her close.

She bit her lip, a grin spreading across her face as she walked with him across the main room and back into their private space. "Must we go to sleep just yet?"

As they entered their sleeping area, the fire was already blazing, the flames lighting up Markos' handsome face just enough for Ocevia to see the warmth in his eyes. He led her to the bed, dropping to his knee as she sat down. Reaching for her foot, he slid her unlaced boots off and set them down on the floor. When he was finished, his green eyes flicked up to hers, glancing at her from under thick lashes.

"What did you have in mind, little one, if not to sleep?"

Ocevia was quiet for a moment, not knowing how to ask for what she wanted. She longed for him to give her everything she'd been missing, his heart and his body, but she realized it would be asking for a lot, possibly more than he was ready or willing to give.

Seeming to sense her hesitation, he rose from his knees and sat on the bed next to her, taking her hands in his. "I realized something as we sat together by the fire," he said as he held her gaze. "In a perfect world, we would take things slow. I would court you. We would fall in love and then I would marry you, build a family with you."

Eyes flicking away, emotions warred inside Ocevia as Markos spoke. Desire, love, longing, and pain. The pain because somewhere deep inside her heart, she knew anything they shared would only be temporary. She belonged to the Sea Goddess, and Miris would stop at nothing to get her slaves back.

When she turned her eyes back to him, a tear trailed down her cheek. "But the world isn't perfect," she said, her voice low.

Markos leaned forward, sweeping his finger across her cheek to wipe away the tear before pressing his lips to hers. His scent, and the slide of his tongue against hers, sent a shiver down Ocevia's spine, the sensation pooling between her thighs. When he pulled away, she was breathless, the intensity of his eyes only taking her breath away more.

"You're right, my sea maiden, the world isn't perfect. Neither you, nor I, live a normal life, but that doesn't mean we can't love each other how we want to love each other. If you're sure about wanting to explore this connection between us, then I want the same. I want you more than I've ever wanted anything in my life, Ocevia. If you feel the same way, then I don't see any reason why we should deny ourselves."

As the firelight flickered in the depths of his green irises, Markos' words enticed her to meet his gaze. Biting her lip, she reached toward him, placing her hand on his shoulder. She leaned toward him, brushing her lips against his.

The kiss was tentative, a question lingering as her mouth left his. As if in answer, Markos slid his arm around her waist and pulled her onto his lap, his mouth crashing onto hers a moment later.

With his arms surrounding her, Ocevia melted into his embrace, fear replaced by contentment loosening her muscles. He tasted like the warmth of the fire, and it burned inside her. It was as though she was being consumed by the flame, but it soothed her more than it hurt. Running his fingers through her hair, he kissed her deeper, his tongue sliding against hers in a sensual dance that sent pulses of pleasure through her body.

The moment he pulled away and pressed his forehead against hers, his eyes darkened, his chest heaving with desire. Her heart pounded in sync with his, her need for him overpowering any hesitation.

"Can I touch you, Ocevia? Would that be okay?" Heart flipping in her chest, she nodded, closing her eyes as her cheeks warmed.

"I want to touch you too." Her voice was barely audible as her cheeks heated even more, a moment of insecurity threatening to throw cold water on the moment. "But I don't know how— I don't know how to please a man. I've never even seen one naked."

Although Ocevia wasn't usually one to become embarrassed, the last thing she wanted was to displease Markos.

Or worse, she didn't want him to decide against claiming her body because she was untouched and inexperienced.

His nostrils flared as he tucked the hair behind her ear and leaned forward to place a lingering kiss on her neck. A breathy moan left her lips and she rocked against his thigh as the touch sent a wave of pleasure into her core. She needed him to touch her there, to show her what it was like to be filled by his cock and writhing with passion.

"There is nothing you could do that I wouldn't enjoy, Ocevia." Trailing kisses down the column of her neck, Markos loosened the ties on her tunic. His deep voice rumbled against her skin as he spoke, puckering her skin with gooseflesh. "My body is yours to touch as you wish. I promise I will enjoy it all."

After spending most of her life wearing no clothes to speak of, Ocevia had always been comfortable in the nude, but it was different with Markos. He would see all of her, would touch all of her, and she wondered if he would be turned off by her imperfections. The way Markos pulled her tunic down her body, however, his eyes taking her in as though she was the most cherished and fragile gift, she realized her concerns were fruitless.

Ocevia's tunic pooled at her waist, her nipples impossibly hard as he trailed a finger down the swell of her breast, his gaze tracking each shutter his touch caused. "You are the most exquisite woman I've ever seen, my sea maiden. *Beautiful.*"

Lowering his face, Markos' hand slid to her breast, pulling the taut peak into his mouth. Ocevia's back arched, nearly forcing her to slide off his lap. She gasped, pleasure radiating out of her core as his tongue circled and sucked the sensitive flesh. Gripping her waist, he steadied her as his teeth tugged gently at her hardened nipple.

"Please," she whispered, her core throbbing for the first time in her life. "I need more."

Chapter 20

LUST AND REVERENCE

With Ocevia in his arms, Markos stood and spun around, laying her down on the layers of fur blankets with gentle hands. Her tunic was still wrapped around her waist, but he crawled onto the bed above her, sliding the loose fabric down her body and dropping it to the floor. Her nipples pebbled in the chilled air, overly conscious of her nudity in his presence.

Gazing upon her body with a mixture of lust and reverence, he lifted onto his knees between her opened thighs, pulling his tunic over his head and tossing it to the ground.

In the firelight, Markos' body was breathtaking, fit for a god. Unable to look away, Ocevia's bottom lip slid between her teeth, her mouth going dry. With the dark stubble on his face, he was the epitome of rugged handsomeness. His pectorals and stomach were sculpted from years of using a sword, the thin trail of hair on his lower stomach dipping into the waistband of his trousers and drawing her attention. A tattoo covered his left pectoral of a broken chain in the shape of a circle, the snapped edges flaring away from each other. As Ocevia leaned up on her elbows, she traced it with her fingers, wondering what it meant, but not ready to ask.

"Can I take these off of you?" Markos asked as he slid his fingers along the waistband of her trousers, the garment much too large for her petite form. Without hesitation she nodded, her eyes never leaving his as his deft fingers unlaced the ties and slid the brown fabric down her hips. Once her bottoms hit the ground, he trailed a finger down her thigh, bringing shivers through her body, warmth building between her thighs.

Falling back on his heels, his eyes roamed over every inch of her, her body tingling with awareness of being so exposed. "You are truly phenomenal to gaze upon, Ocevia."

His words brought a flutter to her chest, the look in his eyes telling her he meant every word. It was something no one had ever told her before, something she'd never even thought about herself. She'd never seen herself as anything but ordinary, no more beautiful than any other mermaid.

Leaning forward, Markos trailed kisses up the flat plane of her stomach, pulling a gasp from her lips and sending her self-conscious thoughts tumbling away.

"Thank you." Her breathy response was drowned out by another gasp as he kissed his way up her body, pulling her nipple into his mouth, licking and sucking. Positioning himself between her thighs, he ground himself against her, his stiff cock straining against the front of his trousers and pressing right where her body wanted him. She writhed beneath him, aching for him to give her more. After a life of being in the cold depths of the sea, the heat of his skin was a shock to her senses, a delicious one.

"Take off your trousers, Markos. *Please.* I want to touch you."

Tasting her lips one more time, his hands stroked her curves as he moved to obey her.

Rising from the bed, he unlaced his trousers, sliding them over his hips. As he stepped out of them, his cock jutted forward, making her mouth water and begging for her touch, but she didn't know how. Having never seen one before, her movements were hesitant.

With his body as bare as hers, Markos crawled back over her, sliding his shaft through her folds as he leaned forward to kiss her again. The touch sent a jolt of pleasure through her core, dissolving any hesitation. She moaned, her heart racing as she reached between their bodies and wrapped her fingers around the thick girth of him. The skin of his cock was silky soft, but beneath that supple surface was solid, hard as stone and larger than she'd expected. She swallowed thickly. Even with as aroused as she was, she wasn't sure he would fit inside her.

A groan rumbling in his chest, Markos fell back on his heels and slowly rolled his hips against her hand, watching as she explored his length.

"Does this feel good, my mate?"

A pearl of liquid formed on the top of Markos' cock as she stroked him, and she leaned forward to lick it, savoring his taste on her tongue. It was salty, reminding her of the sea, but only the good parts. His hips bucked, the air bursting from his lips as he threaded his fingers into her hair.

"Everything you do makes me feel good, little one, but I need to taste you before I explode."

The words sent tremors through Ocevia's body, even though she didn't know exactly what they meant. Everything that had driven her so far had been desire and curiosity. She didn't have enough knowledge about sex to imagine what he could do to her, or how it would feel, but she craved to find out.

Pressing a gentle hand to her shoulder, Markos guided her back onto the bed, the fur soft and sensual against her too-sensitive skin. "Do you still want to do this? There's no pressure to go any further if you aren't ready, little one."

Even though desire laced his tone, and his cock was swollen with need, she knew he meant it. If she wanted to stop, he would have been content with just being together. She appreciated his concern for her comfort, but there was nothing she wanted more than to have all of him.

She nodded, reaching between them to slide her fingers along his length. Her hands ached with the need to touch him. "I don't want to stop."

Gazing into her eyes for a moment, he leaned forward, brushing his lips across hers before he slid down her body, trailing kisses along her chest and stomach. Every inch of her skin was too sensitive to touch, tingling and burning at the same time.

When he settled his shoulders between her legs, he slid his hand along her inner thigh, urging her to open wider for him. She obliged, her core throbbing with the need to be touched.

The cave was dark, with only the fire to provide light, but Ocevia's skin trembled under his heavy gaze. She'd never had anyone so close to such a sensitive part of her body and she was all too aware of how vulnerable she was.

Warm breath brushed across her inner thigh as Markos moved in to kiss her only inches away from where she ached for him. "I've never seen such a perfect cunt, little one. Just looking at it is making my mouth water."

His words sending her eyes back into her head, Ocevia rolled her hips, trying to get his mouth where she throbbed. "No one's ever looked at it be-before."

Her words stuttered, her back arching, as he moved to the other thigh, his breath teasing her in the most agonizing way.

Seeming to enjoy her body's reaction to his sweet torment, Markos huffed a chuckle, only sending more warmth into her center. "Good." He placed another kiss on her leg, this one an inch closer than the last. So close, but not close enough. "I like knowing I'm the only one to see you like this. I would hate to have to track any other men down and pluck out their eyes."

Grinning in the darkness, Ocevia slid her fingers into his long hair, a whimper escaping through her throat when his tongue slid through her folds, lighting her on fire. Her legs fell completely open as he licked and sucked, feasting on her as though she were the sweetest fruit, a groan rumbling from his chest.

"And it's as sweet as it is pretty," he said, the bass of his voice vibrating against her skin.

His tongue moved across the sensitive bundle of nerves at her apex as he slid a finger inside her, working it in and out before adding another. She gasped, her body trembling with the intensity of the sensations he was eliciting. As if her world had been reduced to the feel of his hands and lips on her skin, she clung to him, surrendering to the pleasure.

The muscles in her core tightened as her climax built, her desperation to reach the peak of ecstasy making her grind against his face. He increased the pressure, thrusting in his fingers as he licked and sucked the swollen bud, sending her over the edge and fracturing her into pieces.

She cried out as her body spasmed, her thighs squeezing around his head as he worked her body through the waves of pleasure. Every thought abandoned her mind as she shuddered her release. The only thing that mattered was the man in her bed.

When the aftershocks calmed, leaving her limp and panting, she still wanted more, *needed* more. He crawled over her, his eyes heavy-lidded with desire.

"I need to be inside of you, my sea maiden. *Now.*"

As Markos braced himself over her, ready to claim her fully, her body pulsated with need, her heart hammering against her ribcage. Every cell in her body was on fire, every touch filled with electricity.

Kissing her neck, he trailed his hand down her body, running his fingers through her folds and sending a surge of pleasure through her core.

"You're so wet for me, little one, but are you sure you want to keep going?"

Even as he waited for her response, he caressed her sensitive bud, her head falling back in ecstasy as she writhed against his hand. She wanted him inside her, wanted to feel his touch deep within her, wanted to be one with him.

Wrapping her arms around his neck, she pulled him closer, whispering in his ear. "Yes, I want you inside me. I want to feel you all around me."

Markos didn't hesitate, sliding his hand between their bodies to fit himself against her entrance. With a slow thrust, he slid himself inside her channel, but only an inch.

As the girth of him stretched her, she sucked in a breath, the overwhelming sensation tinged with pain. Allowing her to adjust to his size, his hips remained steady. He leaned forward and kissed her, his touch slow and sensual as her entrance throbbed around him.

"I know this is your first time, Ocevia, and you're so tight. We'll take it slow. I want to give you only pleasure... no pain."

She nodded. Her heart raced and her body trembled, but she closed her eyes, submitting to him as kissed her, pushing his way deeper inside.

After a moment, he began to move, pushing in shallowly and then pulling back, increasing the depth gradually. With his gentle movements and kisses, he coaxed her body to relax and open to him, until the pain had faded, and pleasure replaced it.

"You feel so good." Markos' groan vibrated from his chest as he rolled his hips in and out of her. With each thrust, Ocevia's body trembled, her breaths coming in short gasps.

"Let go, little one," he whispered. "Let the pleasure take over."

As the climax built within her, Ocevia moaned, tightening her grip on him. His own breathing grew heavy as he moved inside her, his muscles tense as he thrust harder, faster, taking her to the edge.

The sensations grew more intense with each thrust, her body writhing as she clawed into his back. Recognizing what she needed, Markos lifted her hips, the new angle hitting the spot inside her that made her see spots. She screamed out as her body shattered, the orgasm ripping through her body, sending wave after wave of pleasure radiating outward from her core.

As Markos approached his own climax, he buried his face in her neck, his movements becoming erratic, every uneven thrust extending into her ecstasy. His body tensed, a guttural groan bursting out of him when he released, spilling his warmth inside her.

A sigh escaped her as he collapsed on top of her, the weight of his body making her feel blissfully fulfilled, their bodies still connected as they lay in post-coital bliss.

With a tender smile, Markos pulled back to look into her eyes. "That was incredible."

Ocevia's cheeks flushed, the feel of his skin on hers still sending shivers across her body. "It was."

Tucking the hair behind her ear, he trailed his fingers down the curve of her face, the touch cherishing. "So, does this mean we're mates?"

Ocevia looked up at him, her breath catching in her throat. "Yes. I think it does."

CHAPTER 21

HOPE IN THE STORM

For the first time in her life, Ocevia woke up with warmth in her heart as her mate breathed softly beside her. She was grateful to be there, in the safety of their shared shelter, as the storm raged outside. She closed her eyes, listening to the sound of the rain, and for the first time in a long time, a sense of peace settled her worried mind.

With no opening to the outside in their small chamber, it was dark in the cave, but the fire still flickered, filling the space with warmth. Ocevia didn't know if it was day, or still night, but she realized they wouldn't be leaving the safety of the cave just yet, not with the sounds of a torrential downpour on the other side of the stone walls.

Rolling onto her back, she watched Markos' eyelids flutter as he dreamed, heat blooming in her core even with the soreness that lingered between her thighs. He'd claimed her as his mate the night before, shared his body with her and gave her pleasure above anything she'd ever dreamed of experiencing. While she wanted to stay there forever, basking in the warmth of his love and never having to leave, she understood that their reality was that of two people from different worlds, and that no matter how hard she wanted it, their love was forbidden, and with Miris seeking them out, it was unlikely they would be able to make it work. Even though she was determined to try, because he was worth everything, she knew they could be discovered, and the consequences would be severe. Though he had promised to protect her and keep her safe, despite the hope she held for their future together, pain still ripped through her chest, telling her that hope was a lie.

Still, when Markos opened his eyes, the green depthless pools of admiration and desire focused on only her, all the negative thoughts were pushed to the back of her mind.

A sleepy grin spread across Markos' lips, his eyes softening with affection as he pulled her close and kissed her.

After their night together, Ocevia's cheeks heated under his gaze. "Good morning." She knew there would be dozens of things she ought to say, but it was the only thought that came into her head.

Markos chuckled and kissed her again, his lips trailing down her neck and shoulders. A whisper of good morning floated from his lips as he nuzzled into her neck. "Just when I thought you couldn't get any more stunning, my sea maiden, you amaze me. How are you feeling this morning?"

A sigh escaped Ocevia as she snuggled closer to him, feeling the warmth and safety of his embrace. "I feel...peaceful...happy." Her voice was barely a whisper, knowing it wasn't the whole truth. There was still a war waging inside her. Before their night together, she had nothing to lose if Miris found her. She would lose everything now. Her very being would crumble if she lost him, and that was terrifying. "Thank you for being here with me."

Markos smiled and kissed her forehead, his hands running up and down her back in a soothing gesture. "I will always be there for you."

As though he'd just noticed the storm, Markos' head tipped up, peering through the darkness toward the leather covering over the entrance to their private space. Upon realizing their companions must have heard what they did in the night, Ocevia's face flushed hot. The sounds of ecstasy they'd made during their night together had been unrestrained.

After a moment, he tucked his face into her neck, kissing her sensitive flesh. "I don't think we'll set out this morning— at least not until the storm clears and the sun dries some of the path."

Ocevia's head fell back as his tongue glided over her pulse. When he pulled away and looked into her eyes, his mischievous grin sped up her heart. "Perhaps we can find something else to do while we wait."

Despite their plans to leave the Arcane camp that day, the severe storm prevented them from doing so. The storm was fierce, with strong winds and heavy rain battering the camp. Over the mountain pass, ominous clouds hovered low in the sky, illuminated by lightning. Because of the storm, any kind of travel was impossible, so the group decided to stay put and wait for the weather to clear.

Following another round of making love, Ocevia and Markos had fallen back to sleep. However, they were awoken later by Aris' voice through the leather screen that served as their door. Since the weather was so terrible outside, the main fire had been moved into a large central cave that could be found by traversing the narrow path along the river at the back of the cave system. Ocevia and Markos made their way there shortly after waking up, the scent of roasting meat drawing them in. For most of the day, the group remained inside the large cave as the storm raged outside, enjoying the communal food and drinks and listening to stories told around the fire.

As day turned to night, Azure and Elios rose from their place around the fire, saying their goodbyes and disappearing into the darkened tunnel that led back to the group's private cave. With a long day of sitting and listening to stories, exhaustion tugged on Ocevia's eyelids, so it wasn't long before Ocevia and Markos, as well as Dimitris and Aris, also headed back.

Walking through the semi-darkness as they followed behind Dimitris, Ocevia nearly ran into the red-haired man's back when he halted mid-step as they approached the area where she and Azure had bathed the night before.

Ocevia couldn't see what was going on in front of him, what had made him stop suddenly, but she heard Elios' sharp voice pierce the silence left when their steps halted.

"You will say *nothing*."

A sinking feeling in her stomach caused Ocevia to step forward, peeking through Dimitris' side just in time to watch Azure shift back into her legs as she slid behind Elios, naked. Unclothed and soaking her tail, her friend probably expected the rest of the group to return later. The two of them stared at each other, but there was nothing they could do. Their secret was out.

Markos tightened his grip on Ocevia's waist, pulling her into him as she twisted the hem of her tunic. While Elios and Markos knew who they were, she realized the other two men may not have been willing to risk their lives for two runaway mermaids, particularly when a goddess was after them. If Aris and Dimitris turned them away, or turned them in, she didn't know what she and Azure would do. Ocevia realized, however, after seeing the look on Elios' face and hearing how he spoke to his companion, that she knew very little about the men in her company. This included the man she considered to be her new mate.

She had shared her body with him but did not even know what he did for a living.

Panic seized her chest as she watched Azure hide behind her lover, trying to make herself smaller. Elios ran his hands through his dark hair, his jaw clenched as he set his eyes on the rest of them. "Make a fire and wait for us. Looks like we all need to talk."

No one spoke as Dimitris dipped his head in acknowledgement and resumed his path through the tunnel and back into the main cavern, Ocevia, Markos, and Aris on his heels.

CHAPTER 22

ELIOS' ADMISSION

Ocevia's heart beat violently against her ribcage as she and Markos followed the other two men into the main chamber of their cave. With his arm around her waist, he leaned over, kissing her on the temple. "It's going to be okay, my sea maiden. Trust me."

Although she nodded, and his words calmed some of the tension in her body, the unknown still filled her with unease. Markos may have trusted his friends, but she didn't know them well enough to feel the same.

Lowering themselves near the fire, Markos wrapped his arm around her waist and pulled her close. Aris added a few new logs, stoking the fire until the blaze doubled in size. Dimitris sat quietly beside them. Both men were silent as Elios and Azure entered the room.

With their hands interlaced, Elios led Azure toward the fire, sitting on the ground and pulling her into his lap. Azure's hands trembled. Her nervousness was palpable, but her lover wrapped his arms around her, clearly trying to ease some of her anxiety.

"I guess I should give you all an explanation." The room was silent as Elios began, the entire group waiting to hear what he would say next. "We're not traveling with human women, as you now know, but I guess I should start at the beginning."

He began his admission without hesitation, telling the group how his ship had gone down and how Azure had saved him. In addition to explaining how women were cursed to become mermaids, he provided details regarding their enslavement and how they were forced to kill in order to earn their freedom.

As Ocevia listened to Elios and Azure's story, her breath halted in her lungs. Bile churned in her gut and threatened to come up. The dread only increased when he told the others of the horrific monster who had saved them when Miris' two scouts found them on the island. He may have been thankful for the kraken, for her, but his descriptions of the creature were terrifying. They reminded her that she was a monster deep down, and she hated it. Twisting the seashell necklace between her fingers, all Ocevia wanted was to crush it and destroy the beast within, but she knew she couldn't. With or without the necklace, the kraken was a part of her. It always would be.

So caught up in her own self-loathing, Aris' voice caught her by surprise. "So, are Azure and Ocevia intending to stay out of the sea for good?"

The answer was complicated, but the question hadn't been aimed at Ocevia, so she remained silent, keeping her eyes on her friend. Azure tucked a strand of hair behind her ear as the rest of the group watched her, waiting for an answer she was probably just as hesitant to give as Ocevia was. She knew neither of them wanted to return to the Lamalis Sea. However, being a mermaid was who they were, so remaining away from the sea forever didn't seem like an option. No matter where they went, Miris would never stop looking. It wasn't in the Sea Goddess' nature to be forgiving.

After a few silent heartbeats, Azure spoke, her voice low and hesitant. "I'm not sure, but I know I don't want to be within the reach of Miris. If she finds us, she'll kill me, and Elios, too. So, the farther we get from her lair, the safer we'll be. Ocevia has never disobeyed the Sea Goddess before, not like I have, so she might survive... after being tortured for running away."

Something within Ocevia crumpled at the words, her shoulders folding inward as she fought the tears that threatened to fall. Not because she was upset, but because she was overwhelmed. The situation they'd gotten themselves into was impossible, and she didn't know how they would survive it. As though sensing her emotions, Markos pulled her closer, placing another kiss on her temple.

"I won't let that happen." There was no hesitation in Markos' voice when he spoke. "Even if I need to take her to another continent, Ocevia will not spend another moment in slavery. Not while I'm still drawing breath."

A smile spread across Ocevia's face as Markos pledged his life for her, but her happiness was tinged with guilt. She knew he meant it, but she'd taken enough lives in her time, and she couldn't imagine taking his as well. If he sacrificed himself trying to save her... she would never forgive herself. Before she had a chance to process anymore of her own thoughts, Markos cleared his throat and continued. "But I do have a confession to make..."

He paused, running his fingers down her cheek, the touch sending shivers across her body. "I already knew they were mermaids. The tribal elder, Great Protector, told me when we arrived. I figured Elios already knew, figured it was why we were running. I didn't want to say anything, out of protection for Ocevia and Azure, not until Elios said something first."

Markos shifted his gaze to Elios. "I was going to talk to you about it, Brother, but I was waiting until we got somewhere more secure."

Lost in his own thoughts, Elios was quiet for a moment, his jaw clenched. It was clear he wasn't happy that Markos hadn't come forward as soon as he discovered the truth, but it would have been hypocritical to be angry when he'd done the same thing.

"I would have said something once we arrived in Ceveasea for the same reason you didn't speak up, Markos. It's not that I didn't trust you, Aris, or Dimitris. We've been through a lot together, and I trust all three of you with my life. But I knew what they were wasn't relevant to our mission, and I couldn't chance anyone finding out who could put them at risk. Anyone at this camp could turn them over for a bit of coin. It was best to hold on to their secret for a while, at least until we got to a safe house."

Seeming to hesitate, Elios pulled Azure closer against his chest. "I suppose there is more I need to explain, at least to Azure and Ocevia."

Ocevia shifted, her attention focusing on Elios as he turned his own to Azure. "I told you I've spent my life traveling. That wasn't a lie, but it wasn't the whole truth either."

It was clear what Elios had to say wasn't easy for him with how he rubbed the back of his neck, as though he was trying to ease the tension. "You asked what The Circle was back at the tavern. Well, Aris, Dimitris, Markos, and I are part of that group. Our mission is to rescue slaves and smuggle them away to the lands where they can live free."

Elios' admission flipped Ocevia's stomach, but not in a negative way. Markos, her mate, risked his life to free slaves. It was why he hadn't batted an eye when being called to protect her and Azure. He'd originally assumed she was another freed slave. In a way, she was.

"And Vasso?" Azure asked Elios, catching Ocevia's attention.

He nodded. "Yes, Vasso and his wife are also part of The Circle, but their roles are different from ours, although no less dangerous. Their inn is used to house freed slaves, and ourselves when we pass through. It also serves as a communication hub for members. The rest of us, more than twenty now, this is our lives. Some of us have been doing this since we were teens. Many kingdoms still support slaveholders, their kings even profiting from the trade, but we do our best to rescue who we can."

Even with all she'd heard, and Markos' hand still wrapped firmly around her waist, there was still a question weighing on Ocevia's mind. "So, what happens to us now?"

Markos stiffened behind her, pulling her closer, but it was Elios who answered. "Nothing changes from here. We'll leave this camp when the weather clears and make our way through the mountain pass to the city of Ceveasea. If we hear any word of Miris' people snooping around, we'll move further inland. Aris and Dimitris will eventually return to Starspell for their next assignment, but I assume Markos will stay with us."

Before everyone turned to Markos, Aris and Dimitris both nodded in agreement. He nodded before her heart had a chance to drop.

"I won't leave Ocevia. There's nothing back in Starspell for me. I can still do my job from inland."

CHAPTER 23

DAMN GOOD WOMAN

As soon as the storm had passed, the sun shone down on the valley, drying up the path they needed to travel on. While the Arcane people had shown them the highest level of hospitality, and there appeared to be no danger in the camp, Ocevia, Azure, and their companions still needed to continue towards Ceveasea. From there, they could seek refuge in the Kingdom of Dekresian, where they hoped to be out of Miris' reach. Even though Ocevia wasn't sure she would ever escape the Sea Goddess' grasp, she had to try- if not for herself, then at least for her friends. While leaving the hidden community to return to the mountain pass posed a risk, they collected their belongings quickly and continued their journey, thanking the Arcane people for their kindness. In order to get to Ceveasea by sunset and far inland before Miris found them, they had to make haste.

Tucked between Markos' thighs on the saddle, Ocevia hugged her cloak tightly around her body. Even with the thick hooded cloak and the clothes given to them by Vasso's wife, the storm had left a chill in the air that seemed to sink into her bones. Maybe it was the temperature, or maybe it was the knowledge of how exposed they were as they traveled through the mountain pass. Ocevia had very little knowledge of the human world, but Markos had told her about the creatures who haunted the area at night, those who fed on the blood of others, and she couldn't help but scan the mountains around them, hoping she wouldn't see an evil pair of eyes staring back at her.

As they continued, the warmth emanating from Markos' body took the bite out of the mountain air. He held her tightly in his embrace, and the steady rhythm of the horse beneath them soothed her. The sun had risen above the mountain peaks, casting a breathtaking golden light on the landscape surrounding them. The mountains towered around them, silent sentinels that seemed to watch their every move. While the sheer drops and rocky cliffs were intimidating, the ethereal softness of the sun accented their magnificent splendor. A sense of awe filled Ocevia, and for a moment, she forgot about her fear.

Halfway to the city of Ceveasea, the group stopped near a stream that intersected their path, allowing the horses to drink and the mermaids to run water over their tails. It wasn't the same as swimming, but it was enough to reset their twenty-four-hour period.

After shifting back to their human legs, they rejoined the men near a patch of grass in order to rest and regroup. The Arcane tribe had given them dried bear meat before they left the camp, so they sat together and ate, chatting casually as a gentle breeze fluttered Ocevia's hair. They couldn't stop for long, not if they wanted to make it to Ceveasea before sunset, but there wasn't an urgency to climb back on the horses either.

As Ocevia sat with Markos in the grass, Aris leaned on his elbows in front of them, allowing her to braid his waist-length golden hair. Azure, Elios, and Dimitris sat nearby, sharing pieces of meat as the men sharpened their swords.

"Have you spoken to Kimon recently?" Dimitris asked after telling them all about a mission in which their friend, Kimon, was involved.

Ocevia didn't know much about Kimon, aside from him being one of their contacts who lived in Ceveasea, but she'd heard his name a few times over their travels. She listened to every word, fascinated by their lives in the human lands. The members of The Circle traveled across the continents and the seas to follow leads and free slaves of all ages, bringing them back to places where they could live in freedom. The men in Ocevia's company were heroes, and just knowing that eased some of the tension in her body.

That wasn't the only reason Ocevia felt more at ease, however. After all that had been revealed around the fire the night before, there were no more secrets between the group about who she and Azure were, about *what* they were. At first, Ocevia had worried that Aris and Dimitris would leave them, or worse, turn them in, but she quickly realized knowing the truth only made the men more protective of her and her friend. This realization lifted a heavy weight off her shoulders.

Turning to his friend, Elios stopped sharpening his blade. "About six months ago. Why? Any recent developments?"

A laugh escaped Dimitris' lips, amusement twinkling in his bright eyes. He hadn't consumed nearly as much alcohol as he had the night before, and it showed in his demeanor. "Do you remember the woman he was seeing? What was her name? Emilia, maybe? Well, our old friend, Kimon, got her pregnant. Word is they've since married."

Ocevia tied a band around the bottom of Aris' plait, patting him on the shoulder to let him know she was done. The moment he moved, Markos scooted closer to her and slipped an arm around her waist. He pulled her into a kiss, Elios' response low in the background.

"I say good for him. We should all be so lucky to have a good woman to come home to. I know that I feel like the luckiest man alive. Once I get my lady to a safe place, all will be right in the world."

"I hope to be just as lucky one day, brother," Dimitris responded, chuckling again.

Sliding his fingers up to cup her cheek, Markos pulled Ocevia's face toward him, his lips only a breath away from her ear. "It feels good to have a damn good woman in my life." He placed a lingering kiss on her neck, sending a shiver through her body.

Grinning, she tilted her head back and looked up at him. "I feel the same way."

He leaned in and kissed her, lingering on her lips, making her pulse quicken.

For a few heartbeats, time seemed to stand still, until Elios' voice disturbed the intimate moment. "Well, we should get back on the move. I don't want these ladies out in the cold mountains after dark."

CHAPTER 24

DANGERS IN THE DARK

O n the border of Avrearyn and the inland kingdom
of Dekresian, Ceveasea was landlocked in the valley
of the Avronis Mountains. Thus, the group would need to
ascend in elevation before going back down into the valley.
With the hope of reaching the city before dark, they set off
shortly after finishing their meal. Though everyone enjoyed the respite from riding, they were eager to reach an
inn so they could rest for a while. Ocevia felt trepidation
as they rode into the unknown, having never been to either
place before. Despite this, she was filled with childlike
excitement. Having a future with her mate and friends in

new places excited her, so long as the Sea Goddess didn't find her first.

Returning to their saddles, they set off in a direction that would take them farther from the sea and Miris. As the sun shone down on them, it made the chill in the air more bearable. The group spurred their horses onward, the animals' hooves thundering across the rocky terrain. As they traveled, Ocevia watched the view ahead for signs that they were nearing their destination.

After traveling the entire day, Ocevia's body was sore from straddling the saddle and she was ready to get somewhere safe. As they rode behind Azure and Elios, she enjoyed sitting so close to Markos and talking with him. Even so, every hour they spent in the mountain pass brought them closer to sundown, and with sundown came the creatures that Markos had warned her about. While night was falling, Elios did not want them to spend the night in a cave in a mountain pass. Because they were close to Ceveasea, he believed stopping for the whole night would be riskier than traveling for an additional hour. With each passing hour, the group pushed their mounts at a swift pace, watching the sunset paint the sky with vivid oranges and purples.

After the sun had set, leaving the mountain pass in darkness except for the full moon, Ocevia's body tensed. With the darkness came a chill, and Ocevia felt the pressure of her uncertain future bearing down on her. Dread crept up her spine as she stared at the cliffs that lined the pass, the lack of sunlight obscuring every cave and crevice as if the abyss had come to watch them. A shudder reverberated through her body as the horses' hooves clapped against the dirt road. The wind whistled through the rocks, a haunting whisper that seemed to follow them with every step. The darkness loomed over them like a living being, waiting to strike at any minute.

"Look." Markos lifted his hand up to point ahead of them as he kissed her cheek.

The warmth of his touch ebbed some of the fear burning at the back of her throat. Looking up, she glimpsed the lights of a city in the distance. Her chest bloomed with hope, excitement energizing her again, but it wouldn't last. As the promise of safety illuminated the sky, Ocevia was filled with a premonition of danger. There was a shift in the air around her, and the mountains went silent. There was a sudden change in mood among the group. There was something coming, but Ocevia was not sure what it was. There was an invisible force in the air that made her wary, and whatever it was, it was coming closer.

The moonlight glowed on the path between the mountains, beckoning those seeking them. Ocevia peered into the darkness, scanning the cliffs on either side of them, hoping her instincts were wrong. As though sensing the same, Elios slowed his horse's pace in front of them. As he scanned the shadows for an unseen threat, his hand moved to the hilt of his sword.

"I need you to take these." Markos' voice was barely a whisper as he slid the reins into her trembling hands. She gripped them tightly, struggling to calm her breathing. Markos shifted behind her, his arm leaving her waist before silently sliding his sword from its scabbard. Before she could comprehend what was happening, a shrill hiss pierced the night air, sending ice through her veins. They weren't alone.

A bone-chilling hiss seemed to come from everywhere at once as Ocevia and her companions moved through the mountain pass. As Ocevia and Azure sat helplessly in the saddles, all four men held their swords at the ready, scanning the shadowed cliffs. Azure whispered a question to her mate, but Ocevia couldn't hear the words over the beating of her heart. Something was watching them, even if she couldn't see it. With how the horses' tails flickered with agitation, it was clear they felt it too.

Dimitris whistled, drawing their attention as he tipped his head to the left. Before Ocevia's eyes could focus on the shadows enough to see a form in the blackness, massive wings flapped over their heads just before a dark form swooped low, nearly knocking Elios off his horse. Azure ducked forward, shrieking as her mate swung his sword at the beast. The creature's flight back into the darkness made it clear he'd missed.

A moment later, chattering echoed in the air around them, making it seem as if dozens of the creatures were hiding among the shadows. As Ocevia held her breath, she twisted her head to see where the creature had disappeared. As the air swirled around them, another flying creature emerged from the shadows, aiming again at Elios. This time, the sound of his sword slashing through its flesh was unmistakable, but the beast didn't fall. With a pained scream, its wings carried it back into darkness.

As she watched her friend fight the creature, Ocevia's body trembled, and the thought that there might be more lurking in the shadows filled her with burning dread.

Making a hand signal in the air, Elios' urged his horse to pick up speed. As Azure held onto the reins, fear pinching her features in the moonlight, Elios pulled his legs up below him, standing on the saddle. The movement was so smooth, Ocevia could not believe what she was seeing. Moments later, Markos kissed her on the neck, rising behind her as Storm picked up the pace. Despite the horse's fast progress along the path, her mate braced himself in the saddle, his boots secured in shoe holds she hadn't noticed before. There was no doubt the four men had done this maneuver many times before, perhaps when rescuing slaves.

As Ocevia watched her mate in awe, Dimitris whistled again, signaling another warning just before a dark form dropped down from the side of the mountain. It collided with Aris as he stood on his horse, knocking him off. The sound of his body hitting the ground ripped Ocevia's heart from her chest. She turned to look behind them, watching as his attacker landed on the ground beside him. Aris lay motionless on the ground as the humanoid figure slowly rose to its full height, tucking its wings into its back.

"Fuck. Aris." Dropping into the saddle behind Ocevia, Markos grabbed the reins and urged Storm to turn around.

Ocevia's heart pounded as Markos urged the horse into a gallop, heading back the way they had come. As they raced toward their fallen friend, Dimitris leapt off his horse and sliced his blade across the creature's throat. Its head struck the ground with a thud. Behind them, Elios fought against another one of the creatures, slashing across its stomach. It hit the cliff side, its body slumping to the darkened ground below.

As soon as the second creature died, the air around them went silent. Markos guided Storm to where Aris was lying on the ground, Dimitris hovering over him and checking his injuries. With bated breath, Ocevia watched as the blond-haired man lifted his head, speaking to his friend. She thought he was dead, killed trying to save her, but he wasn't. Aris was alive.

With a torch in his hand, Markos wrapped his arm around Ocevia's waist as they watched Dimitris check on Aris' injuries. It was clear their friend was in pain from the expression on his face. However, he remained stoic through it, not crying out to avoid attracting more predators. The mountains around them were calm, but they still needed to find a way to start moving again quickly and get Aris to a healer. Even though the danger had passed, Ocevia was still shaking, and Markos pulled her to him, caressing her arm. Elios and Azure approached as they waited, drawing Ocevia's attention. Her friend was clearly shaken, just as she was, but appeared uninjured. With the chaos that had just unfolded, it was a small miracle that only one person from their group had been harmed

"His leg is definitely broken," Dimitris said, his voice filled with concern for his friend. "He may have a few broken ribs, too."

Elios moved forward and crouched beside Dimitris, the two men discussing how to get Aris to the city, when moving him could cause more injuries.

Noticing her friend stiffen, Ocevia realized the creature's severed head lay precariously near Azure's feet. Neither woman noticed it before, with all their attention focused exclusively on Aris' well-being. Wanting to see more closely, she nudged Markos toward her friend.

A head of black hair rested in a pool of blood on the dirt. Using the tip of his boot, Markos maneuvered the creature's face toward them. With a disgusted gasp, Ocevia buried her face in her mate's chest, her eyes taking in its appearance even though she knew it would haunt her nightmares.

The creature's translucent skin stretched over angular bones as its crimson irises stared sightlessly up at the night sky. Elongated teeth protruded from its pale gums, sharp enough to rip flesh from bone. Its hands were stained with dried blood, its claws curved and razor sharp. The creature looked human, but it was twisted into something... *evil*. Just like her.

Shivering, a deep sadness washed over Ocevia as she thought about what the human being it had once been must have gone through to become such a monster. She had her own darkness, a part of her that she had to fight every day. A part of her Markos didn't even know about. Sensing an odd kinship with the creature, she turned away. She wasn't ready to confront her own darkness yet, and she knew if she stayed any longer, she would be tempted to succumb to it.

"Blood sucking piece of shit." With a swing of his boot, Markos kicked the severed head toward the cliff. It hit the rock with a splat, disappearing into darkness.

Their attention was diverted from the vacant spot on the ground to Aris' hiss as he tried to stand up, Dimitris and Elios supporting each shoulder as he did so. Leaving Ocevia's side, Markos moved toward his friends, helping them lift the injured man onto Dimitris' horse. Aris slumped upon the saddle in pain. His jaw was clenched as he held tight with one arm and used the other to wrap around his middle. A moment later, Dimitris mounted the horse too, sitting behind Aris and helping to support his weight to keep him steady as they rode away.

Returning to Ocevia's side, Markos wrapped his arm around her waist and led her back to Storm. Just as he lifted her onto the saddle, she watched Elios attach Aris' horse's reins to his own. Once everyone was secure in their saddles, the group returned to the pass, heading toward the city of Ceveasea at a brisk pace. There, they could get the medical help Aris desperately needed and find safety. At least for a little while.

CHAPTER 25

CEVEASEA

Although tensions remained high for the rest of the trek toward Ceveasea, the group reached the border without further attacks. Ocevia exhaled a deep breath when they stepped onto the main street, relief giving her lungs permission to expand freely. The illusion of safety didn't last, however, because something about the city seemed off. She scanned the streets, the eerie silence sending a shudder through her.

In contrast to Starspell, which had been alive with nightlife when they paddled into the harbor, Ceveasea was still. No patrons lingered near the taverns and inns, no carriages or travelers moved along the sidewalks. Except for the candles lighting dozens of windows, the city appeared deserted. Even the stars in the sky seemed muted, as if they, too, knew it was not safe to be seen in the dark.

"Where is everyone?" Azure asked, her voice and the clapping of hoofbeats the only sounds breaking the silence.

"The citizens know what lives just outside their borders, and they're smart enough to avoid them. Unlike Starspell, you won't find many people out in the open here after the sun goes down."

Even though Ocevia had seen the creatures herself, Elios' words sent a chill down her spine. It was impossible to believe that a city of that size would shut down at dark for any reason. Remembering what lived in the mountains behind them and realizing how exposed they still were, she shifted on the saddle. Until they were inside a structure, they weren't safe.

Markos nuzzled into her neck and pulled her closer. "You don't have to worry, my sea maiden. We're almost there."

As she leaned back against her mate, watching each shadowed alcove they passed, Elios led them toward a side street. Toward the end, they came across a stone structure with a large gate built into its side. A man stood just inside of it, staring out at them. His appearance caught Ocevia off-guard, sending her heart plummeting, but the men in her group didn't seem surprised to see him. A moment later, he nodded and opened the gate, the squeal of the metal hinges slicing through the silent darkness.

"Staying for long, Elios?" he asked, closing the gate behind them.

With a lantern in one hand, he untethered Aris' horse and led it toward the stable at the back of the enclosed space, not waiting for an answer.

"We're not sure how long this time, old man. Do you have a few rooms for us? Say, three?" Elios replied in a playful tone, as if he knew their new host well.

"Aye." Tending to the horses, the older man didn't even glance at them as he spoke.

Sliding his arms from around Ocevia's waist, Markos dismounted and helped her down. She stepped to the side, standing next to Azure as she watched him lead Storm into the stable. Upon his return, Markos, Elios, and Dimitris helped Aris down from the saddle and carried him to the back door of the building.

"Is Phaedra inside, Georgios?" Markos asked, reaching for the wooden door. As Aris' friends supported his weight, his face was twisted with pain, only filling Ocevia with more guilt.

Georgios nodded and waved his hand toward them. "Yes. Yes. She's inside."

Passing through the wooden door, Aris was carried through a storeroom and into a long corridor, Ocevia and Azure following behind the men with their hands interlocked. They were silent as they made their way down the hallway, their footsteps echoing through the narrow space. Near the end of the hall, a single lantern rested on a small table and barely illuminated the dark wooden walls. The air in the corridor seemed too thin, the building just as devoid of life as the city itself. Georgios claimed someone named Phaedra was inside, but Ocevia didn't see or hear anyone.

Near the end of the hall, they stopped in front of a set of double doors. Shifting Aris' weight to the other two men, Elios knocked before crouching down and sliding something beneath the door.

Almost immediately after Elios slipped a small item beneath the double doors, a woman with dark, curly hair opened them. For a moment, her large green eyes studied them, the deep scar across her cheek intensifying her gaze. Then, with a nod towards Elios, she stood aside and allowed them to bring Aris into the room, placing him on a large table.

"What happened to him?" Phaedra asked as she removed Aris' clothes with a dagger.

Elios pulled out his own dagger and assisted in removing his friend's clothing. He tossed the shredded trousers to the ground, leaving Aris' body on display. Bruises had already developed around his midsection, and his right leg was bent at an odd angle. Clearly in pain, Aris' eyes opened briefly before rolling back into his head. Ocevia and Azure stepped back, guilt turning Ocevia's stomach.

Even as she stood to the side, Ocevia noticed the bronze medallion Phaedra had laid on a small table. Its central symbol, a broken chain, was identical to the tattoos on Elios, Markos, and Aris' chests. Even without seeing him shirtless, she knew Dimitris probably had the same symbol on his pectoral. It seemed to be the symbol of The Circle, the group whose sole purpose was to free those who were enslaved.

"Vampires. A few of the evil beasts attacked us on our way into the city. Knocked him off his horse," Elios responded.

Phaedra shook her head as she drew out a vial of shimmering violet liquid, her expression full of dread. "Was he bitten?"

"No." Without hesitating, Elios opened Aris' mouth, allowing the healer to squeeze a few drops of the liquid onto his tongue. The two of them checked Aris' injuries, as if they had been working together for years. Dimitris, Markos, and Ocevia moved out of the way, settling on a settee against the wall. A moment later, Azure joined them, her stunning face lined with worry. Although Ocevia could tell her friend had something on her mind, the moment was too tense to interrupt, so she remained silent.

"He just fell from his horse? His left leg is broken, a few ribs as well. No signs of head trauma, but probably some internal bleeding. A few broken bones wouldn't be enough to make this big man pass out."

It was clear, from the robotic way she worked, that Phaedra had dealt with vampire attacks many times before and was unphased by them. After wrapping his ribs, she attached a board to the broken leg to keep it straight. While it was a relief they had reached a healer in time to save Aris' life, Ocevia knew the healing process would be challenging. Leaving Ceveasea to travel further into the mountains would almost certainly mean he would be left behind, and that sent an ache through Ocevia's body. She didn't want their little group to split after all they had already endured.

As soon as she was done, she washed her hands and pulled out a set of keys from her apron. "You three can carry him into the sickroom across the hall. Then I'll show you to your rooms." Phaedra gestured toward the double doors. "Will you be staying long, Elios?"

As soon as Elios moved toward Aris to do as Phaedra asked, the rest of them stood, Markos and Dimitris moving forward to help their friend. "We'll be here for a while," Elios said as they carried the unconscious man back into the darkened hallway. "Thank you for your hospitality, Phaedra, and for your discretion."

CHAPTER 26

THE DUSTY LANTERN

The Dusty Lantern Inn and Tavern served many purposes in the city of Ceveasea. It turned out that Phaedra was a well-known healer, and the infirmary she had at the back of the tavern was the place most people sought when they needed such services. At night, however, the building was silent. With there being no patrons on the first floor of the structure when they'd arrived, since the tavern closed at sunset, Ocevia hadn't realized they were in a tavern until they'd ascended the stairs to the second floor.

Being watched over by Phaedra and unable to walk on his own, Aris was set up in a small room across the hall from the infirmary. It wasn't much; just a single bed and a table for supplies against the wall. She and Georgios, her husband, promised to watch over him as the rest of the group rested. Ocevia and Markos followed Phaedra and the remaining members of their group up the creaky wooden stairs to the second floor of the stone building, where there was a line of guest rooms on either side of the darkened hallway. Once shown to their rooms, their host disappeared down the stairs with a promise to return with dinner and beverages. After everything that had happened to the group since leaving the Arcane River tribal camp, they hadn't eaten in hours. Ocevia's stomach was empty.

"Do you want to take a bath while waiting for dinner?" Markos asked as he closed the door behind them, wrapping his arm around her waist and pulling her close. "The tub isn't large, but it's deep enough to soak your tail."

As compact as the guest quarters were, Ocevia wasn't surprised that the tub was small. She wasn't disappointed either, however. Having a private bathing room and bathtub was a small blessing.

Leaning into his strong body, she nodded. "A bath sounds nice...if I have the energy to shift. Today has been overwhelming." It had been more than overwhelming, but she didn't want to make the day's trauma about her.

"You'll feel better after a hot bath and a good night's sleep." He kissed her forehead, sliding his hand up and down her back. "Aris will be okay. We will all be okay."

Markos' words sent warmth through her, but Ocevia couldn't ignore her worries. There were too many, and they were too deep-rooted. Even being so far from the sea, she knew Miris could reach her. Still, the last thing she wanted was to allow the Sea Goddess to continue to rule her life. She'd done that for long enough.

Brushing his lips across her cheek, Markos slipped his arm around Ocevia's waist. He led her toward the bathing room, guiding her down onto the stool. As she sat beside the tub, he turned on the tap, holding his hand below the water stream to check the temperature. It still fascinated her how humans had found a way to bring water into their structures, to clean the salt out of the water so it was clean and clear.

"Thank you for taking care of me." Reaching over the lip of the tub, Ocevia dipped her hand into the warm water, excitement trailing down her spine to the tips of her toes, her tail begging to be free. She needed to get into the water, even if she couldn't fit her entire mermaid form into the tight space.

Wasting no time, she tugged at the laces of her tunic, still not familiar with human clothing. Markos grinned, batting her hands away and taking over. The front of her tunic fell open with a slip of his hand, exposing her breasts to the chilled night air. His fingers brushed the taut skin of her nipple, the touch sending a surge of desire into her core. She gasped, arching her back into his touch. His other hand snaked around her waist and pulled her close, his lips finding hers with a softness that made her knees weak. Their passion ignited a flame between them, and she surrendered herself to it.

When he pulled away, his green eyes burrowed into hers, stilling her breath. Markos trailed a finger down her cheek, touching her as though she was the most cherished gift. "It's easy to take care of someone when they're your everything."

Slipping her trousers to the floor, Markos lifted Ocevia from the stool, placing her in the bathtub's warm water. Her legs shifted into a stunning turquoise tail a moment later, its size forcing the fin at the end to drape over the side of the tub. It didn't matter. The water felt amazing. When she lifted her gaze to her mate, his eyes were wide, watching her with utter amazement. He reached forward, sliding his fingers across her tail.

"You truly are exquisite, my sea maiden. A work of art."

Even though her cunt was tucked away in her mermaid form, it still throbbed within her, wanting to be touched the same way he touched her tail.

"Our appearances are deceiving. We're meant to allure men. You're simply under my spell."

Her voice lilted with the last sentence, her tail lifting in the air to accent her words. What she didn't want to remind him of was that her beauty and sensuality were curses. If she remained fully human for the rest of her life, her appearance might not have been as appealing.

A huff of a chuckle escaped Markos' lips and he leaned forward, pressing his lips to hers. She closed her eyes and savored the moment, allowing herself to forget the burdens she bore. His touch was a reminder of all that was good, and she wanted to stay in the moment for as long as it lasted.

When he pulled back, his mouth turned into a grin. "Your beauty is a blessing, not a curse. And all of you is beautiful, not just your flesh."

Reaching out, he cupped her face, his fingers tracing the contours of her cheekbones. "You are a masterpiece," he said, his voice soft and filled with affection. "And I'm honored to be able to see you for what you are, to have a chance to love you."

A knock at the door interrupted the tender moment. Kissing her once more, Markos stood, leaving the bathing room to answer the door. Georgios' raspy voice met Ocevia's ears only a moment before the aroma of a home-cooked meal met her nose. Her stomach rumbled, reminding her of how hungry she was.

Squeezing a dollop of soap into her hand, she washed her hair while Markos carried the tray of food and wine across the bedchamber, setting it on the small table near the wall. She rinsed the soap from her hair, watching Markos pour their wine as she finished bathing, no longer wanting to linger in the bath. Although the water felt amazing against her skin, exhaustion tugged at her eyelids, and she wanted to taste whatever meal was steaming in the covered dish on the table.

Shifting her tail back into her legs, Ocevia stood, water dripping down the curves of her body. Markos re-entered the bathing room with a mischievous grin on his lips, his eyes devouring her body. After stepping out of the bathtub, a flush tinted her cheeks as she moved toward the fluffy white cloth he held.

A shiver swept through her as he ran the towel over her, taking in her body with his heated gaze. Wrapping the towel around her, Markos pulled her close. Sparks of electricity flowed through her veins as his lips brushed against hers. She leaned into him, her heart racing as his hands roamed her body. In a moment of pure bliss, Markos pulled her closer, deepening the kiss. His touch consumed her, setting her body on fire, giving it life like it never had before. For a moment, time seemed to stand still.

He slowly released her, his hand lingering on her skin as he gazed into her eyes. Their dinner's herbal scent wafted through the air, making Ocevia's stomach grumble loud enough for Markos to hear.

"Are you hungry?"

Ocevia and Azure had dreamed so many times of eating human meals again, describing their flavors and smells as they bit into flaky pieces of dried fish, but none of them could prepare her for the real thing. The first bite of the meat and vegetable stew was like an explosion for her taste buds, and she couldn't hide her moan.

Markos chuckled, seeming amused by her exaggerated reaction. "My goal from now on will be to find the best foods in the land so you can moan in pleasure when you bite into them."

As heat flooded Ocevia's face, she shoveled a chunk of fresh bread into her mouth, its buttery goodness sending her eyes rolling back. Savoring the flavor, she chewed slowly. "I support this idea. There are a lot of meals I need to eat to make up for the time I lost."

Each bite was better than the last. The meat and vegetables melted in her mouth, complemented by a thick gravy seasoned with just the right blend of herbs and seasonings. When they finished eating, Markos put their plates away and placed their tray outside the door. Ocevia had not yet tried the wine, however, so he kept it. Because she didn't like the wine in Starspell, she didn't think this one would be any different. Water was still her drink of choice, even after she had left the sea.

A hungry expression adorned Markos' face when he returned to the table, but he wasn't hungry for food. Butterflies fluttered in her stomach as he lifted her from the chair, pulling her into a kiss as he held her. While clinging to him, she parted her lips, letting his tongue explore her mouth, licking and tasting. Her head spun as he deepened the kiss, the taste of wine and spices. She melted into him, her entire body tingling as his hands traced her curves, leaving trails of heat in their wake. His lips never leaving hers, Markos walked her to the bed, setting her down on the soft mattress.

"I'll be back," he said before disappearing into the bathing room. Sounds of water splashing met Ocevia's ears as she waited, fighting to keep her eyes open even though her body wanted him. Only moments later he returned, his hair wet, water trailing down his toned chest and dipping into the towel wrapped around his waist.

"You smell so wonderful. I didn't want to get you dirty."

His grin was purely mischievous as he sauntered to her, untucking the towel around his waist and allowing it to fall to his feet. Ocevia's teeth tugged at her bottom lip as her eyes locked on his cock, stiff and jutting toward her proudly, begging to be touched.

Reaching out, she slowly curled her fingers around his length. Breath caught in his throat, his eyelids flickering closed as he savored her touch. She stroked him gently, exploring every inch of his hardness. A low moan escaped his lips as his body shuddered, his breathing quickening.

A mixture of pleasure and longing dominated his expression as he opened his eyes and met her gaze. As she increased her speed, his hips bucked against her hand, his breath coming out in short gasps.

Her thoughts of their night in the cave sent a thrill through her and she wanted nothing more than to please him. Leaning forward, she fed his cock into her mouth, wrapping her lips around its head and sucking him in. As his orgasm built within him, his body tensed, his breathing coming in short, ragged gasps. His hands moved to her head, guiding her up and down his shaft, pushing her to take him deeper into her mouth. Thrusting forward, tremors rocked him as his orgasm hit his body, her name like a plea on his lips.

CHAPTER 27

BLISS

Waking up the next morning in a warm bed with Markos' strong arms wrapped around her was a dream Ocevia never thought would come true. The sun's rays streamed in through the slender windows, illuminating the dust particles dancing in the air. She watched them as she cuddled into Markos' side, the beating of his heart against her ear bringing a smile to her lips. Love filled her heart, bursting at the seams. He'd worshiped her before falling asleep, exhausted and sated. Just thinking about it created a flutter in her belly, desire building as she turned to gaze at his face.

When she turned to look up at him, his emerald eyes looked back at her. His lips curled up in a smile that stirred her very soul. She leaned in, kissing him softly as Markos snaked his arm around her waist and pulled her closer. "Good morning, little one. How did you sleep?"

Ocevia smiled, a contented sigh escaping her lips. "I slept very well." She nuzzled closer, seeking his warmth and comfort. "I'd rather not leave this bed."

Markos chuckled, his chest vibrating beneath her ear. "You don't have to." Tucking her hair behind her ear, he leaned forward and kissed her forehead. "After everything you've been through, you deserve rest."

As she smiled against his chest, thoughts of what she had been through intruded upon their moment, stumbling into her head. The arm around her waist tightened, and Markos pulled her on top of him, the blanket sliding off to reveal her naked body. With how he looked at her as though she was the most beautiful thing in the world, she didn't shy away from showing him her body. She enjoyed seeing his body just as much.

Markos leaned forward and kissed her, his lips caressing hers with a tenderness that made her heart swell. With reverence, his hands explored every inch of her body. Sparks of pleasure coursed through her veins as he touched her, making her body come alive. Gasping, she opened her lips, allowing his tongue to explore her mouth, deepening the kiss.

As their kiss became more intense, Markos rolled her onto her back and positioned himself between her legs. A moan escaped her lips at the sensation of being filled with his thick hardness as he entered her slowly. Clinging to him, she felt his heart beat against her chest as they moved in perfect harmony. Like a dancing wave, his movements were slow and gentle, filling her with pleasure. They moved together as if they were one, connecting at a level she never thought was possible.

As his hands moved lower, his fingers found her sensitive bud and rubbed small circles, sending pleasure coursing through her. She gasped, her hips arching to meet him as a wave of pleasure washed over her. As he increased his tempo, he kissed her neck, licking and nibbling her skin. Her body quivered with pleasure, and as he increased the intensity, her orgasm built. With a cry of pleasure, her body tensed and then released, sending her into a blissful state of euphoria as Markos followed her over the edge. He collapsed onto her, his breathing heavy and ragged. They lay there, their bodies still intertwined, as they slowly recovered. Markos rolled to the side and pulled her close, pressing a tender kiss to her forehead. Despite her racing heart, she smiled and snuggled into his embrace.

Before Ocevia climbed out of bed that morning, Markos had already gone downstairs to message a friend about a safe house. When the house was ready, they would move there where they would be safer than in the tavern. Upon his return, they went downstairs to the tavern for breakfast together.

In the tavern, Dimitris was already seated at one of the tables, chatting with Georgios as the older man placed a cup of brown liquid in front of him. As he drank from the cup, Dimitris turned his gaze towards them. "You're just in time for coffee."

Markos guided Ocevia to the table and pulled out her chair for her. As soon as she was seated, he kissed her on the cheek and pushed her closer to the table. "I'll be back shortly."

A moment later, he crossed the room to the bar, where he spoke quietly to Georgios. The bar owner nodded and they both disappeared into the kitchen.

"You make him happy."

Ocevia was so engrossed in watching her mate that she nearly forgot Dimitris was across from her. With the words warming her cheeks, she smiled. "He makes me happy too."

In the dim light of the restaurant, his eyes sparkled. "That's all that matters."

Before she could respond, Markos returned and sat beside her at the table. Georgios followed behind him, setting breakfast plates and mugs of coffee on the table. Despite the bitter smell, Markos lifted it to his mouth and drank deeply. As he placed the mug back on the table, he thanked the bar owner and then turned to Ocevia with a smile. "I hope you're hungry. It's the finest breakfast in town."

Just as she lifted the spoon toward her mouth, Azure and Elios walked in. They sat down, and the bar owner immediately dropped two more plates of food and mugs of coffee onto their table. Even though he had a grumpy disposition, the older man was certainly proficient at his job.

"How's Aris?" Elios asked, taking a bite of his meal. Having never had porridge before, Ocevia wasn't sure about the texture, but the taste was pleasant. Turning her gaze toward Elios, she ate another spoonful.

"He's in a lot of pain, so Phaedra has been administering a relief tonic often, which makes him tired. He's asleep now," Dimitris responded. By the way they interacted, it was clear he and Aris were good friends. There was a close bond between all four men.

Aris' pain unsettled Ocevia's stomach, but she shoveled a scoop of eggs into her mouth regardless, the taste reminiscent of her childhood. Although she couldn't recall much, she was certain her mother had fed her eggs. While the memory threatened to send her into a downward spiral, she managed to return her attention to the conversation.

"Anyone send a message to Kimon?" Elios asked, shoveling the eggs into his mouth faster than Ocevia thought possible.

Markos placed his utensil on the plate and dipped his head. "This morning. Told him we're here and received a response a short while ago. The safe house will be ready for us tomorrow. I'm not sure if Aris will be ready to move yet, though. One of us may need to stay behind with him. I hate to leave his care to Georgios and Phaedra while he's so injured. Phaedra can care for him, but he's too big for her to lift on her own."

Before speaking, Dimitris lifted his coffee mug and took a sip. "I'll stay with him if need be. You two should get these ladies to the house when it's ready. They'll be more comfortable there- and safer."

As if toasting Dimitris, Elios raised his mug. "Thank you for offering, brother. But I can't help but wonder if you're only willing to stay behind to sample the drinks in this fine establishment."

It was impossible for Ocevia not to giggle, and her friend did the same.

"Those drinks won't be on the house either," Georgios said from behind the bar. "I'll have your ass washing dishes."

Rolling up his napkin, Dimitris tossed it at Elios, the ball landing near his plate. "Ha, ha. Funny, really." He looked over toward the bar. "Not you, old man. I'll wash dishes if you need help. It's better than washing Aris' ass." With a smirk on his face, he returned his eyes to Elios. "Anyway, what's on the agenda for today, boss?"

Elios leaned back in his chair and wrapped his arm around Azure's shoulders. The sight of her friend cuddling against her mate's side, their blossoming love evident on her face, warmed Ocevia's heart. "I would say to remain hidden, but we need ears on the ground in case Miris' people show up asking questions. I don't want to be blindsided."

The mention of Miris chilled Ocevia's blood, but Markos' lips brushing her cheek eased the dread. "I'll go speak with Phaedra about reaching out to our contacts in the city. I'll be back soon."

Seeing her mate walk away, Ocevia couldn't help but want to follow him, just to stay close to him, but she didn't. As she turned back toward her friends at the table, Azure sat down in the chair Markos had just vacated. Her friend's expression was mischievous. It made her miss the times when they used to spend time together, talking and pretending their lives weren't cursed.

"Well..." Azure's tone was teasing as she dragged out the word, making Ocevia blush.

"Well, what?" With the other men at the table, Ocevia didn't want to talk about her private moments with Markos. However, from the way her friend wiggled her eyebrows, it was clear she wanted to know everything.

"Tell me how all of that happened." Azure pointed in the direction Markos had gone. "No judgment, of course. Elios and I got together fast as well. I'm just curious."

Her friend's questions only intensified the flush on Ocevia's cheeks. Looking around the room, she made sure her friends weren't paying attention to what they were saying. So caught up in their own discussion, they weren't paying the two any mind. Turning her gaze back to her friend, Ocevia blew out a breath. "From the moment I saw him standing outside the tavern, I knew he was mine. I couldn't deny my interest in him. I wanted the chance to see what we could be."

"I felt the same way when I saw Elios clinging to those rocks after the shipwreck. Out of everyone that night..." As Azure glanced at the other side of the table, she lowered her voice slightly. "Out of everyone who died that night, he fought so hard to survive. I couldn't take my eyes off him. It felt like a sign. Like I was meant to find him. I may have carried him to that island, but we saved each other."

As she sipped her drink, Ocevia reached for her friend's hand, needing physical contact. Despite the love Markos gave her, her heart was still tumultuous. There was a deep fear in her mind that she would be found and dragged back into the sea. "Do you think we can get away with this? I mean, actually get away with it. I can't help but feel like Miris' eyes are on us everywhere we go. I don't want to go back, Azure. I can't leave Markos."

Something flashed across Azure's eyes, a shadow that suggested her mind was also troubled. She squeezed Oce-via's hand. "I would be lying if I said I wasn't worried. All I know is that these men will stop at nothing to keep us safe. We should find some comfort in that."

CHAPTER 28

VANISHED INTO THE DARKNESS

Following breakfast, Markos and Dimitris scoured the city to weed out any rumors that they were being followed and to gather supplies. Azure, Ocevia, and Elios remained downstairs when they left, Azure and Ocevia helping Phaedra care for Aris, while Elios helped Georgios around the bar. With the potential for Miris' people traveling to Ceveasea to find them, it was safer for the runaway mermaids to remain in the back rooms of the structure and away from public view. Throughout the morning, Aris slept, but Ocevia kept an eye on him in hopes of relieving some of her guilt by taking care of him. With the magnitude of his injuries, the healer kept him medicated with a pain tonic that knocked him unconscious for hours at a time. When he awoke, however, Ocevia helped him adjust his position and even fed him breakfast.

With the bar's opening approaching, Azure joined Elios in the kitchen to prepare food for them and for the guests. Markos and Dimitris returned shortly thereafter, as patrons filled the tavern. With hooded cloaks masking their appearance, Ocevia and Azure sat with Elios in the shadowed back corner of the tavern. Markos and Dimitris mixed in with the crowd, listening to conversations. When the crowd finally vacated the building as the sun set, the five of them helped Georgios clean up.

Aris unexpectedly entered the room seated on a chair with wheels as Ocevia wiped down the tables, drawing her attention. Although she'd never seen anything like the contraption he sat in, she smiled seeing him up and about, her chest heaving with relief. Leaving the rag on the table, she crossed the room to where everyone had gathered around him, sliding her hand into Markos'.

"How are you feeling, brother?" Elios asked, patting his friend on the shoulder.

Despite wincing as he rubbed his leg, Aris' smile remained. "Pretty good, considering. My leg and ribs hurt like hell, but I'm glad to have this rolling chair." He gripped the wheels on the side of the chair and maneuvered it a few inches back and forth. "Phaedra had Georgios bring it in from storage. I can't get up the stairs, but at least I can make it to the bathroom by myself. Having someone help me piss does little for my warrior image."

It warmed Ocevia's heart to see him try to lighten the mood, despite being so injured. After fearing he would die of his injuries, there he was in front of her, cracking jokes. It only made Ocevia like him more.

"A person helping you piss is the closest you can get to having someone touch your cock," Dimitris said, handing Aris his ale and sitting next to him.

The injured man took a sip of the ale with a smirk on his face. "Guess I'm lucky you were around to help me out then."

Dimitris chuckled, nearly spitting out his own drink. "It's the least I can do for a friend. Just be glad I'm not asking for anything in return." He clinked his glass against Aris' and winked.

Trying to stifle her laughter, Ocevia pressed her face against Markos' cloak sleeve. Having taken care of Aris all day, Ocevia was glad to not have had to help him to the bathroom. Phaedra and Georgios had taken over when those moments came, saving Aris and the females from embarrassment. However, Dimitris seemed keen on teasing him.

While everyone examined Aris' rolling chair and spoke with him, Azure slipped out of the room, heading to the bathroom down the lantern-lit hallway. Moments after her friend disappeared into the darkness, a wave of dread swept over Ocevia and the tavern echoed with the sound of broken glass. *Something was wrong.*

While icy horror cemented Ocevia's body to the ground, the world seemed to move in slow motion. Elios' grin fell as his body twisted. Without a word, he dropped his drink to the ground and ran in the direction Azure had gone.

A second later, Markos turned to her with a strained expression. "Stay here with Aris. I'll be back."

Before she could respond, he disappeared into the darkened hallway behind Dimitris. Abandoning his work inside the kitchen, Georgios returned behind the bar, wiping his hands on a towel. "What's going on? Is something wrong?"

Ocevia turned to face him but words failed her, unable to admit her greatest fear had come to fruition. She didn't know what had just happened to her friend, but her body told her there was something wrong, even though she couldn't see into the hall.

Just as the back door slammed, she bolted toward the hallway in a rush of adrenaline. Through the broken latch on the metal gate, all three men disappeared from the stable and into the night. Despite knowing the vampires waited patiently for prey to leave the safety of their dwellings, Ocevia followed them.

The night was eerily quiet. The only sound was the occasional hoot of an owl, its call echoing throughout the darkness. The stars, however, shone brightly, twinkling in the night sky like a thousand tiny fireflies. There was a sense that the world was holding its breath, waiting for what was going to happen next.

"Markos. Please wait! The sound of her boots echoed through the night as she moved toward the main street. Her heart hammered against her ribcage and she slunk back as a figure approached her from down the block. Stopping in her tracks, her breath caught in her throat. The figure moved closer until she could make out Markos' face in the dim light. Exhaling a sigh of relief, she took a step forward, calling out to him.

"Ocevia, I told you to stay inside where it's safe." His voice was unyielding, but his touch against her cheek was soft.

Gripping his arm, she shook her head. "I won't stay inside if you're looking for my friend. Where is she, Markos? What's going on?"

For two hours, the group searched the city for Azure in the darkness, but the trail was cold. Ocevia could not smell her in the wind. It seemed as if she had disappeared altogether.

After returning to the tavern, Markos, Ocevia, and Elios mounted their horses and galloped into the mountains while Dimitris remained inside to watch over Aris. They knew there were dangers at night, but none wanted to wait until morning. Her friend could be back in the sea by then, ripped apart by Miris.

As they traveled south at a high rate of speed on the mountain pass, Ocevia leaned forward on her saddle with Markos' arms tightly around her. Even if she wanted to talk, the horses' hooves clapped loudly against the packed dirt of the road, making it impossible for her to do so. Due to the threat of another attack, she did not wish to raise her voice too loudly.

After several hours of traveling, they arrived back at the Arcane River tribe's camp, and were forced to stop and rest. Even though Elios didn't want to stop, the horses couldn't continue anymore, and neither could they. Unlike the first time they visited the Arcane tribe, the trio did not spend time socializing or drinking at their fire. Grabbing food and drinks, they retired to the same cave they'd stayed in before. By the time she soaked her tail, Markos bathing alongside her, Ocevia could barely keep her eyes open long enough to return to their bed. The two of them were asleep within minutes after climbing into bed.

As Ocevia drifted off, her last thought was of Azure. She hoped her friend was safe, and that she could survive until they found her.

CHAPTER 29

LOSING HOPE IN THE STORM

As they stepped outside into the cold morning air, the sun was just rising. Ocevia breathed deeply, the crisp air energizing her senses and waking her from her sleep. Taking little notice of the tribal camp around her, she followed Markos and Elios to the stable to get their horses.

Her mind was occupied with her friend's absence, leaving her with no space for anything else. There was no doubt in her mind that the same was true for her companions.

Having refilled their water bottles and dried meat supplies, the trio set out a short time later, hoping the weather would remain favorable until they reached Starspell. A hint of gray clouds was visible in the distance, but the sky was clear. Still, the air was heavy and cold, indicating a storm was coming. There was a faint scent of Azure on the breeze, telling Ocevia they were going the right way, but she knew there was a chance her friend was already dead. The thought threatened to rip her heart from her chest, but she pushed it away, repeating in her head that they would find Azure before it was too late. It was the only outcome she could accept.

"It's going to storm soon." Her senses were stronger than humans, but she could tell Elios knew the same by the clench of his jaw. As he turned toward the darkening clouds, his features tensed even more. The horses maneuvered skillfully through the rocky terrain, their hooves pounding against the ground. On this part of the mountain pass, they had to move slower, despite the urgency of their journey. The terrain was too treacherous for them to travel as fast as they had the night before. Even as the ground beneath them shifted and swayed, Ocevia remained steady on the saddle with Markos' arms around her.

Markos pulled her closer to his chest as she sat on the saddle in front of him, kissing her on the neck. "Hopefully, we can beat it. When we get out of this area, we'll pick up the pace again."

Pulling her cloak tight around herself as the breeze chilled her bones, Ocevia nodded. It was all they could do to reach Azure. If they were forced to stop, Azure and her captor would be allowed to get even further away.

The brine of the Lamalis Sea reached Ocevia's nose two hours later, but they were still hours away from Starspell. As the wind picked up, the smell of rain filled the air. Ocevia glanced upwards, noting that the dark clouds had grown more viscous in the distance. The storm was getting closer, and they would have to hurry if they were to reach Starspell before it hit. It was either that or find a place to shelter. She knew Elios didn't want to stop. Neither did she, but the weather didn't seem to be giving them an option. As rain began to fall, thunder rumbled in the distance, making the horses restless. Spurred on by the increasing wind and rain, Elios and Markos drove their horses faster through the rocky terrain. Their hooves pounded against the hard ground and splashed through puddles as they moved quickly. Thunder grew louder, and lightning flashed in the sky as the storm intensified. The winds picked up, whipping Ocevia's hair and cloak around her. Elios and Markos had a tough time keeping the horses under control as they whinnied, and their movements became erratic. Rain pelted down, soaking them to the bone and making it difficult to see the way ahead. Ocevia gritted her teeth as the storm's energy surrounded her, the wildness of its elements coursing through her veins, sending her heart into a furious rhythm and triggering her primal fight-or-flight response.

With another roar of thunder, Storm reared back, bucking and nearly throwing Ocevia from his saddle. Elios was forced to recognize defeat and detour into the valley, seeking shelter in one of the many large caves along the cliff walls. While waiting out the storm, Azure would get further and further away, but they could do nothing about it. All they could do was hope her captor had been forced to stop as well, leveling the playing field.

Unlike the Arcane River tribe settlement, the cave they hunkered down in did not have a hot spring to soak in or comfortable beds to sleep in. The air was miserably cold, making finding remnants of a fire left behind by another traveler a lucky find. Although it would not burn for long, there were enough logs left for them to dry out some of their clothes and skin.

As Elios got the fire started, and Markos set up a space in a dry corner for them to sleep, Ocevia slipped outside the cave, sitting in a large puddle and shifting into her tail. She'd swam in storms before, hunting for souls and damning the innocent to the sea, so sitting in the rain was something she could endure, but there was still something ominous about it. Guilt flooded into her as the rain hit her body with a torrential force that nearly threw her onto her back. Having caused so much harm, she knew she deserved the punishment. Taking the beating of the storm as a punishment for her actions, she closed her eyes and let out a deep sigh. Despite the thunder reverberating around her, she sat there trembling. The storm was a reminder of her mistakes, her guilt, her regret, and her pain. She knew she had to find a way to make amends and move forward, no matter how hard it may be. The first thing she had to do, however, was save Azure.

Just as tears burned the backs of her eyes, Ocevia stiffened her spine and shifted back into her human form, returning to the safety of the cave. Even though she was forced to kill, never taking a life voluntarily, the penalties of her crimes still haunted her. Whatever her circumstances, she could never escape the things she'd done, which only reminded her that she wasn't good enough for Markos. She didn't deserve love or happiness.

"We'll find her, little one." She'd been so caught up in the downward spiral of her mind, she hadn't noticed her mate approaching her. Markos slid his arm around her back, leading her toward the small blanket he'd laid out in the back of the cave. The small fire flickered, the blaze uneven and threatening to burn out. As Elios stood before it, he draped their cloaks over a boulder. With nowhere else to turn, Ocevia allowed Markos to guide her to the ground.

Sitting beside her, he gently lifted her chin, gazing into her eyes with such compassion that she nearly broke down in tears. He kissed her forehead, whispering against her skin. "We'll get through this together."

"If Miris gets her, she will—." Warm lips pressed against hers in the middle of her statement, silencing her words. She melted into the kiss, her heart still racing. Her fear and sadness melted away for a moment as they kissed, and she forgot about the storm and the danger they were in. In that moment, it was just the two of them, and she felt safe and loved.

Markos pulled away, searching her eyes for a moment before speaking. "We will find her and keep you safe. You will never be a slave again."

Although his voice was filled with conviction, she knew it wasn't something he could promise. Fear still raced through her veins, regardless of how much she wanted to believe him. A sad smile tugged at one side of her mouth. It was all she had to offer. She knew he was trying to reassure her, but she had been a slave for so long that she had learned to be wary. The only thing she could do was take it one day at a time and hope for the best. Happy endings were so rare for people like her.

CHAPTER 30

RETURNING TO THE SEA

The storm took many hours to pass, leaving them trapped in the cave for the entire day and night. Despite having spent most of her life sleeping in uncomfortable places, Ocevia slept fitfully, her dreams flashing from nightmare to nightmare. The more the storm raged, the more her mind replayed the same horrors over and over. Even when she opened her eyes, death and destruction still haunted her mind.

With the ground still muddy and difficult to traverse, the trio set off on the mountain pass late morning. Their hope was that the dark clouds in the sky were remnants of the storm that had passed, and not an omen of a new one. The group traveled in near silence, the moment too hopeless to talk about trivial things. Ocevia sat nestled between Markos' thighs on the saddle, her senses searching for Azure in the wind but only smelling rain and mud. Even the brine of the sea was a faint memory in the thick air. Azure had already entered the water. The thought roiled Ocevia's stomach, dropping it into the depths of despair, and every fiber of her being told her it was true.

As they neared the sea, the scent of the sea grew stronger, and Ocevia's heart beat faster. Almost as if a string was attached to her chest and tying her to the sea, it yanked and tugged her forward.

Cresting the final high point in the pass, the city of Starspell appeared in front of them like an oasis, the sparkling waters of the Lamalis Sea sending a shiver down Ocevia's spine. Her fingers twisted painfully in the reins, the need to leap from the horse and dive into the depths to find her friend nearly impossible to resist.

"We'll need boats," Elios said, his voice catching Ocevia by surprise. He hadn't spoken for most of the journey, but the tense expression on his face suggested he'd been deep in thought. His love for Azure was undeniable, and he was equally concerned about finding her as she was. After Azure saved him, they were life mates, and that bond would last a lifetime.

"Vasso will know where to find them. We should head to the tavern." Elios nodded at Markos' suggestion, urging his horse to move faster.

As the sun set over the sea and they moved through the back alleys of Starspell, the despair inside Ocevia heightened. Even though she was so close to finding Azure, it felt like she was still miles away. As the orange and pink hues of the sky contrasted with the ominous clouds earlier in the day, Ocevia felt a glimmer of hope.

She took a deep breath, letting the salty air fill her lungs, stealing her resolve.

"I need to get into the water. I'll be able to smell her in the current. I'll be able to find her." Her words tumbled out, but there was nowhere for her to go, not while the horse was still moving.

Markos tightened his hold on her, tucking the hair behind her ear. "Let us find a boat first, little one. I know you want to find your friend but going back into the water by yourself will only get you captured as well. We'll go together. Elios and I may not be able to swim below the surface like you, but we can at least fight above the water if we need to, and you'll need a boat if Azure is injured."

He looked into her eyes, his expression serious. "We can do this, but we must be careful. I don't want to lose you too."

As Ocevia fought the pull of the sea, the process of getting boats was a blur. Thankfully, Vasso had access to multiple sailboats, and despite the moon being high in the sky, they were able to take two of them out to sea. As Elios manned his own craft, Markos and Ocevia sailed alongside. The wind blew in their favor as they followed the channel Ocevia knew would lead them to Miris' underwater palace. Her gut told her that's where she would find her friend.

It was a dark night, but the stars sparkled in the night sky, reminding Ocevia of how Starspell got its name. In the darkness over the sea, the stars brought an enchanting glow to the city. The waves lapped against the boats as they silently sailed through the night. The sails creaked in the wind and the oars splashed as the trio paddled to move the two boats faster. As each mile passed, Ocevia wanted to abandon the boats and swim to find her friend, but she didn't want to leave Markos behind. At night, the mermaids hunted, and she could already hear their song in the wind. There was no way she could leave Elios and Markos. Not until the sun was in the sky and the mermaids retired for the day. Even putting her own scent in the water could put them all in more danger.

"Are they out?" Markos' words cut through Ocevia's concentration, drawing her attention to him as he sat behind her, the paddle moving in his hand.

The burn of shame filled her chest as she nodded, knowing what he meant, even if he wasn't saying it. It was her kind, mermaids who killed, that he was referring to. "I hear their song, but they're not close to us. If we keep moving southeast, we should be able to avoid the main channel."

Sailing only a few feet away from them, Elios cleared his throat. "How far from the main channel is Miris' palace? That's where she is, isn't it?"

Ocevia nodded, holding the paddle still. "Close to a day by boat, but I can't be sure. Even without being in the water, there's still a faint scent of her rising from it. Whoever took her, brought her through here. It's likely she's in Miris' dungeon." Blowing out a breath, her face dropped. "The Sea Goddess will punish her but she won't kill her. She's too valuable."

As she said the words, the doubt in them burned her tongue. When Miris was angry, she was unpredictable, as well as powerful. There was no way to guarantee she wouldn't kill both for their forbidden acts and for their disrespect. There was no way to guarantee Miris wouldn't kill them all. In the Sea Goddess' mind, Elios' soul already belonged to her, and Markos' soul would only sweeten things.

The thoughts caused Ocevia's hands to tremble, the oar slipping and clattering against the floor at her feet. Scanning the water, she hoped not to see a mermaid's dark shadow break the surface.

She turned back to look at her mate, whose green eyes reflected the moonlight. While swallowing back the dread that rose in her throat, she turned her gaze back toward Elios. "She won't kill me and Azure, but she will kill you both. You need to turn around and let me go in alone. It's too dangerous for men to be on the sea at night."

Elios was already shaking his head before her words had even finished leaving her mouth. When she turned to Markos for support, his head shook as well. "How many times do I have to tell you, my sea maiden? Only death could make us leave you to do this alone, and neither of us intend to die tonight."

CHAPTER 31

INTO THE BELLY OF THE BEAST

After a long journey through the sea, they finally reached the surface near Miris' underwater palace the next afternoon. They'd traveled all night, with only dried meat and waterskins. The men had their weapons but even those didn't ease Ocevia's churning stomach. There was an entire world below the surface filled with dangerous creatures that could attack them in the boats before they even knew to wield a blade. Setting his paddle down on the floor, Markos slid forward, wrapping his arm around Ocevia and turning her to face him. Undeniable fear twisted his features as his lips pressed against hers, the goodbye lingering just on the fringes of their reality. There was a chance she would never return once she dipped below the surface, but neither of them was willing to admit it.

Ocevia savored the moment, relishing in the warmth of his lips against hers and the strength of his embrace. They both knew it could be the last time they were together, and the thought made her heart ache. As her tears fell, Markos wiped them away, his eyes shining with emotion when she pulled away. With one final lingering kiss, Ocevia slipped over the side, shifting into her tail as she held onto the side of the boat.

Markos moved forward, covering her hands with his. "You'd better return to me, my sea maiden, so I can show you true freedom." Reaching down, he wiped a tear from her cheek. "I love you."

Numbness crawled through Ocevia's body, making her limbs weaken. For a moment, she debated crawling back into the boat, but couldn't. Her best friend was in trouble and needed her help.

With a heart wrenching *I love you*, she let go of the boat, allowing her body to sink below the surface.

Ocevia's tail propelled her swiftly through the water, the coolness of the depths doing little to ease the tension in her body. She swam past schools of fish and coral reefs, the light from the surface gradually fading away. Despite the darkness, she pressed on, determined to return to the boat before nightfall. She couldn't leave her mate and Elios unprotected when the mermaids began their hunt again. Her powerful tail moved her through the water with ease, and before long she could make out the distant silhouette of the Sea Goddess' palace.

Spires of pink and blue coral reached up from the ocean floor, the sun's distant light filtering through them and creating an ethereal glow. The palace was a marvel, a testament to the skill and craftsmanship of the merpeople.

Since she had been to the palace before, she vaguely knew the layout, but she didn't know where the dungeon was. She did know that the entrance was guarded, however. Hiding behind a cluster of coral, she watched as the guards patrolled. Four mermen moved through the underwater courtyard, passing in front of the pressurized entrance that allowed the inside of the palace to remain waterless. Her heart raced as she watched the guards, her body trembling with nerves. Getting caught would prevent her from saving anyone. It would be the end for her.

As the guards moved toward the outside of the grounds, Ocevia left her hiding spot, swimming with subtle movements so she wouldn't draw attention. When she reached the entrance, she entered quickly, activating the switch that drains the water from the compartment. Within mere moments, the chamber dried and Ocevia dropped to the ground, shifting her tail back into her legs. Taking one last look behind her to make sure she hadn't been seen, she crept through the next set of doors, and into the castle foyer.

After grabbing a large vase from the entrance room, Ocevia crept down one of the corridors that appeared to lead into the lower levels of the palace. While she moved as close as she could to the wall, no one stopped her. There had been a guard in the foyer, standing in front of double doors, but he never turned in her direction. It had almost been too easy, making her wonder when her luck would run out.

When she reached the bowels of the palace, the dank mildew smell made her nose wrinkle. The faint sound of dripping water somewhere near her made her wonder when the sea might reclaim the space, but she pushed those ominous thoughts behind her and kept moving. She descended deeper and deeper into the dungeon, the walls slimy and wet. There was a chill in the air that grew more intense with every step.

Steeling herself, she swallowed hard. The torches set in the walls flickered, emitting an eerie glow, and the stones beneath her feet were slick and uneven. To avoid slipping, Ocevia grasped onto the algae-covered wall, but it offered little support. There was an oppressive feeling in the air, as if the walls and stones were watching her. With the icy fingers of fear tracing up her spine, she quickened her pace, eager to find Azure and get out of there.

The shuffle of feet and the clanging of keys caught her attention as she approached the intersection at the end of the corridor. Her luck had run out.

Pressing her back against the wall, she tried to remain hidden in the shadows as she heard the guard's footsteps growing ever closer. She held her breath as she waited for the guard to pass, her hands shaking around the large vase. The light of the guard's torch illuminated the walls as he got closer, making her heart skip a beat as she remained still and silent. As the shadow turned into the full frame of a large male, she blew out a breath, swinging the vase with all her strength.

Ceramic shattered as the large object hit his head, dropping him to the ground with a resounding thump. Rushing forward, she grabbed his torch, taking the keys he held.

"Hello? Is someone there?"

A female's voice came from one of the dungeon cells, her tone pleading. Ocevia moved forward without a thought, stepping over the unconscious guard.

"Is someone there?" The voice echoed through the darkened corridor again, leading Ocevia to one of the metal doors on the right. She could see a figure through the small window on the door, but couldn't tell who it was. Her fingers trembled as she tried key after key until she found the one that worked and unlocked the door. When the door swung open, the rusty hinges squealing, her heart dropped into her stomach. There was a female inside, but it wasn't her friend.

Against the far wall, a red-haired female stared at her for a moment before closing the distance between them. She peered out the open doorway, her eyes going wide when she saw the guard's unconscious form on the ground.

"Who are you? Are you here to rescue us?"

Following the crushing blow of not seeing Azure behind that door, it took Ocevia a moment to respond. "I'm looking for my friend, Azure. Who are you?"

"My name is Corileia. Your friend is here. I've healed her." Without a thought, Ocevia turned and fumbled with the keys to open the next cell.

Before she slid the key into the door, the healer placed a hand on her wrist, halting her movements. "Before I let you open the door, I have to warn you. Your friend is in bad shape. She has been tortured relentlessly."

CHAPTER 32

ESCAPING THE LABYRINTH

The key trembled in Ocevia's hand as she slid it into the metal lock, unlocking the metal door to Azure's dungeon cell. No sounds reached Ocevia's ears from the other side of the door. If Azure was inside, she wasn't screaming for her rescue, or beating on the door to get attention. The air in the space thinned, making it difficult to breathe as the metal door slid open.

In the corner of the dark room, a figure crouched in the corner, the lantern barely illuminating the cell. Battered and bruised, Azure was a shell of her former self. Ocevia sucked in a breath, taking a step into the room.

"Azure?" Keeping her voice low, she glanced down the corridor, ensuring the guard was still unconscious. He was. "I'm here to get you out of here."

Blinking rapidly, it took a moment for Azure to rise to her full height. When she did, she crossed the room quickly, cupping Ocevia's cheek. "You're really here. I don't understand. How did you get past the guards? Where is Elios? Everyone else?"

Ocevia glanced over her shoulder again, a smirk spreading across her lips, still not believing she'd knocked the large male out. "I clocked the guard outside over the head with a vase. He dropped hard. I snuck past anyone else I saw, but there weren't many guards on the way here. I guess they figure you can't get out of this cell, anyway. I caught a glimpse of Corileia in the cell next to you and let her out. Elios and Markos are in boats on the surface, waiting for us to return."

Eyes widening, Azure shuffled on her feet, her anxiety palpable. "Ocevia, we have to get Elios out of here before Miris realizes he's here and captures him."

Reaching for her friend's hand, Ocevia nodded. She had the same fear. "No one's coming. Let's go. Corileia, do you know the way to get out of here?"

Although she'd found the dungeon, it had happened by chance. The palace was a labyrinth, and she didn't trust herself to find the way out. Taking a step forward, the healer nodded, indicating they should follow.

No guards passed the three females as they made their way through the dark halls of the palace's lower levels, but Ocevia knew there would be guards near the entrance.

She'd seen them when she entered and was lucky none caught her.

Adrenaline surged through Ocevia as they navigated the passages leading them through the palace, her heart beating too fast, but she did her best to calm herself. They were so close to freedom and she couldn't let her nerves get them caught. When they approached the end of the corridor, the candlelit foyer before them, they stopped so she could peer around the corner. "There's one guard standing between us and the exit. We are going to have to take him out."

Having already taken out one guard, Ocevia's pent up energy told her she could do it again. Her friend, however, was weak. Azure swayed on her feet, the shadows around her eyes showing her exhaustion. Still, she nodded.

With the guard's back to them, the trio crept out of the passage. Corileia reached for a fire poker as Ocevia lifted another vase. Moving silently as wraiths, they approached the unsuspecting guard. Without hesitation, Ocevia swung the vase, hitting him across the back of his head. He fell to the floor a moment later, the gash on the back of his head oozing blood. There had not even been a moment to feel guilty about what she'd done. Instead, they rushed toward the airlock chamber, pushing the button to fill with water.

The moment the airlock opened, the three females, already in their mermaid forms, surged to the surface. Azure, who was injured and exhausted, swam faster than Ocevia thought possible. It hadn't taken long before the first of Miris' guards began to pursue them. Ocevia picked up her speed, her friends following close behind. The guards weren't close, but they were gaining on them.

A blast of Miris' energy swirled the water around them, sucking them back down toward the seafloor. Clenching her teeth, Ocevia swam against it, her body already aching from its pressure. The seashell necklace around her throat hummed with energy, demanding her to free the beast. If she did, she could get rid of the guards and save her friends. Turning her eyes up toward the surface, where she knew her mate was waiting for her, she halted, her heart breaking at the decision she was making.

Another surge of Miris' power slammed into them, pulling them back. Azure turned to look at Ocevia, her eyes wide with alarm at whatever she saw on her friend's face, but Ocevia had made up her mind. Pointing toward the surface, she nodded, urging her friend to keep pushing forward. Without another word, Ocevia turned and swam back toward the guards.

Through the turbulent water, no less than six guards swam toward her, the blades in their hands reflecting the sliver of light reaching the depths. Ocevia turned to look behind her, making sure Azure had continued to the surface, before pulling the necklace off her neck.

Ancient power surged through her body as the kraken roared within her, forcing a silent scream from her lips. She flailed her arms, allowing the beast to take over her body as the guards got closer. In the corner of her eye, she thought she saw Corileia swimming beside her, but her vision blurred as the monster within her warped and twisted her body, sending eight tentacles ripping from her flesh.

Turning toward the approaching guards, rage burned inside the creature. Ocevia's own emotions were overshadowed by what had taken over her body. Her mate and her friends were simply shadows in her mind. Her sole focus was on the mermen below her, the taste for blood too strong to fight.

Throwing her tentacles out behind her, Ocevia surged toward the guards. The three below her twisted away from her, swimming back toward the palace to escape her. The beast inside her cackled, the chase only increasing its pleasure. It only took a moment for her to catch up to the three guards, wrapping her tentacles around them and ripping them apart, tasting their blood and roaring into the abyss.

The scent of mermen caught her attention as they swam above her, heading toward the surface. Roaring again, she twisted and sped toward the surface. There were no thoughts of her friends or the boats they waited in, as her giant bulbous head breached the surface of the water. She plucked four mermen from the water and pulled them back below the surface.

Struggling in her grip, the guards stuck her with their daggers as they fought for her life, but it did them no good. Her rust-colored skin was thick and there was too much fire raging in her veins to notice pain. Pain only enraged the beast more. Propelling herself back into the depths, the kraken ripped the mermen apart, tossing their dismembered bodies to the seafloor below.

As the kraken reveled in its kills, tasting the blood of its victims, another surge of Miris' power swirled the sea around her, catapulting her downward. She stretched her tentacles around herself to right herself, just as the Sea Goddess emerged from the darkness below.

CHAPTER 33
THE IMPASSE

T he Sea Goddess threw up her arms, a curse on her lips as she swam toward Ocevia's kraken form. The bolt of energy hit the water around Ocevia, stinging her flesh as she tumbled to the side, losing control of her monstrous body. The creature roared in pain, its tentacles thrashing wildly as the Sea Goddess shouted another silent incantation into the water. A powerful spell churned and roiled the dark water around them, shaking the very foundations of the ocean. Once the water settled around her, her tentacles still twitching from the spell, Ocevia turned to look for Miris.

When the next wave of power came, she was ready. With her tentacles thrown out behind her, she surged toward the source of the spell, ignoring the sting as she sought out her attacker. When Miris' dark hair came into view, the kraken that held Ocevia's body didn't think. Surging forward, it gripped Miris in its tentacles on instinct, its suction cups latching on to the Sea Goddess' torso and tail, squeezing her until she could barely move. Miris' face contorted in pain as she screamed, but it was muted by the water surrounding them. With her arms pinned at her sides, Miris was helpless, unable to wield her magic, and there was no one nearby to save her. Trying to free her hands from the kraken's grasp, she struggled in Ocevia's tentacles, but they squeezed tighter as the beast moved toward the surface. There were still guards in the water, and Ocevia needed to make sure none attacked her friends. In the kraken's scattered thoughts, it was the one thing they both agreed on.

Lifting Miris out of the sea, the kraken's giant head breached the surface, a scream drawing its attention. Two males and a female stood in two boats, floating a mere hundred feet from where she floated. In kraken form, it took a moment for Ocevia to register what she was seeing, but when she did, her eyes locked on her friend. Standing near Elios, Azure's hand covered her mouth, the horror on her face shredding Ocevia's spirit within the confines of the monster. She never wanted her friends to know what she was. The last thing she wanted was for them to fear her. Although she wasn't sure if Azure recognized her, her instincts told her she did. While Ocevia wanted to flee, her body did not move. She felt like she was rooted in place, unable to escape, her kraken form preventing her from speaking.

"Call off your dog, Azure!" Miris' voice sounded unhinged as she struggled to get free. "Or my guards will destroy every one of you!"

Angered by the Sea Goddess' statement, the kraken thrashed its tentacles in a violent fit, slamming her down below the surface before pulling her up again. Miris' silver tail twisted in her grip, nearly slipping free, but the suction cups on Ocevia's tentacle held on to her. When Ocevia's eyes returned to her friends in the boat, a shrill cry bellowed from her giant mouth.

Lucia stood behind Markos, a scowl twisting her feral face as she held a dagger to his throat. Although the mer-bitch covered his mouth, fear showed through his wide eyes, filling the kraken with desperate panic. Her mate was in danger and she needed to save him. Not knowing how to do that, she remained still, not wanting to provoke Lucia.

For a moment, the world was silent, as Ocevia watched the fear in the eyes of the man she loved. Turning her eyes to Miris, the Sea Goddess' lips lifted into a cruel smile before narrowing her eyes to Lucia. A heartbeat later, with a slight nod of the Sea Goddesses' head, Lucia grinned, slicing Markos' throat and tossing him into the sea.

Agonizing rage clouded Ocevia's vision as Elios jumped into the sea behind her mate's body. Her wails pierced the air, her tentacles gripping either side of the Sea Goddess' body and ripping her apart. Tossing the pieces of Miris' body away from her, Ocevia dove below the surface, desperate to find her mate.

Blood colored the water as Markos drifted toward the sea floor, gripping his throat with his hand as if trying to stop the bleeding. Even though he fought, Ocevia knew the wound was fatal. The sight of him trying to survive ripped her heart from her chest. The beast cried out, the sound sending a ripple of power through the water as it reached for Markos.

With his body held securely in her tentacles, Ocevia returned to the surface, hesitating only for a moment before approaching one of the boats and setting him down. He choked and sputtered as blood poured out of him and soaked into the wooden bottom of the boat. Pain like none she'd ever felt splintered Ocevia's chest. The beast's body trembled, barely able to contain the onslaught of emotions. Elios and Azure floated in the water nearby, watching her but too afraid to approach. Not knowing how to save him, she knew she had to move out of the way and let her friends try.

Knowing her friends feared her only hurt more. With another look at Markos, Ocevia dipped below the water, moving out of the way so her friends could help her mate. Despair sent her plummeting to the seafloor, everything in her wanting to give up. However, a new power hummed in her veins, telling her to return to her lover, that there was still a chance.

Holding the necklace firmly in her tentacle, Ocevia's kraken form warped and twisted, the beast returning to its cage as she shifted back into her mermaid form. The moment her turquoise tail reappeared below her waist, she darted back toward the boat, breaking the surface right next to where her mate lay dying.

Seeing Markos' life pouring from his unconscious body as she held onto the side of the craft, Ocevia screamed, shifting her tail into her legs and climbing into the boat. She wrapped her arms around her mate as Elios held pressure against the wound, but it wasn't enough. His heart was no longer beating, breath no longer expanding his chest.

Leaning over his body, Ocevia's breaths came out in sobs, the pain of her loss threatening to shred her insides, but as though her touch was filled with magic, the bleeding stopped. The world was silent as Ocevia pulled away, watching the wound knit itself back together in front of her eyes.

"I don't understand." Her breath coming out in ragged gasps, Ocevia kissed Markos' cheek. As she watched color return to his face, air whooshed out of him, his eyes fluttering open to look at her. She smoothed the damp hair away from his face, still not understanding what was happening, or how it had happened. The strange power within her still tingled as it moved through her body, but she had no time to process the cause as Azure spoke.

"Ocevia." Her friend's tone was questioning, but Ocevia didn't respond right away, afraid of what she had to say. There were too many thoughts in her mind, many too overwhelming to think about, but her mate needed her attention.

Ocevia muttered, not turning her eyes away from Markos, whose neck wound had completely healed.

"Ocevia... was it you who killed Miris?"

Body stiffening for a moment, Ocevia let out a deep breath, her voice low as she continued to gaze at her lover.

"I wanted to tell you for a long time, but I accepted this form, to protect the world from what I really was." Sorrow filled her eyes as she turned to look at her friend. "I didn't want you to fear me. I didn't want anyone to fear me."

Swallowing thickly, Azure met her gaze, her expression sincere. "I wouldn't have feared you, Ocevia." Seeming distracted, Azure placed a hand on her shoulder, looking out toward the sea. "Ocevia, where's Corileia?"

Shaking her head, she reached forward to cup Markos' cheek. His eyes were still open, but he seemed dazed by his ordeal. "A guard took her. He took her back to the palace. I was going to go after them but then I saw Miris and..." Ocevia drifted off, pain squeezing her lungs. "I couldn't know for sure that you wouldn't have turned away from me if you knew, Azure. My own family feared me."

As a tear slid down her cheek, Markos reached up and wiped it away with his thumb. "Are you okay?" he asked, his expression warm with deep affection as he looked at her.

A small smile tipped up the side of Ocevia's mouth as she nodded. "All that matters is that you are okay, Markos. That everyone is okay."

Azure sat on the floor beside them, speaking beside Ocevia's ear. "Ocevia... if you killed Miris, that means—"

Azure choked back a sob as she raised her hand to her mouth. As Ocevia turned to face her, her half-smile didn't meet her eyes.

"I know what it means."

Sliding his hand up to cup her cheek, alarm showed in Markos' eyes. "What does it mean, Ocevia? What's going on?"

Even though her insides were spinning in chaos, the truth of her situation finally hitting her, Ocevia tried to mask her own worry. She slid her hand into Markos' as the other caressed his cheek. "It means that I'm the new Sea Goddess."

EPILOGUE

"**I** just want to ensure that I understand your orders correctly, Goddess Ocevia. I only live to serve you."

Sitting on the step in front of Ocevia's throne, her messenger, a merman named Nestoras, scribbled on a piece of parchment.

Ocevia blew out a breath, ready to return to her residence after a long day of ruling over an underwater kingdom that continued to shrink. Having already freed Azure from her life debt, she realized all the mermaids deserved the same freedoms. "My people are no longer forbidden from going into the human lands. They can visit their families and friends as often as they would like. If they want to be free from the curse completely, however, if they no longer want to have the ability to shift, they will need to come to the palace. I have to touch them to lift the curse."

As fast as his pen moved, she hoped he got the declaration correctly, but she didn't ask. Being an effective ruler required delegating tasks to those who could carry them out efficiently, so she had to trust him to do his job right. After another moment of scribbling, Nestoras shifted his turquoise gaze once again to look at her. "And the souls, Goddess Ocevia. What about the collecting of souls?"

Her skin tightened in annoyance at his question. She had only told him the answer fifty times already. As she narrowed her eyes to him, she hoped the fifty-first time would be the one to stick. "Mermaids are no longer collecting souls. Miris used their energy to enhance her power and beauty. I have no desire to make others sacrifice their lives for me."

After meeting with Nestoras, Ocevia returned to the palace's private chambers, her eyelids heavy with exhaustion. It had not been an easy transition to become the new goddess. Despite inheriting Miris' magic when she'd killed her, some within her ranks still needed convincing. From the moment she ascended the throne, it had been a constant struggle. Now that she was freeing the mermaids from their chains, support for her had grown.

Running her fingers across the gilded walls as she walked, Ocevia stopped in front of a set of large brown doors. They opened before she could touch a handle.

Bright green eyes met hers, Markos' smile bringing a flutter to her stomach. After she brought Markos back from the darkness of death, he was given the ability to transform into a merman, allowing them to live below the sea together. The scar remained on his neck, a blatant reminder of what Lucia had done to him before Azure killed her. He was not cursed, and he was not obligated to stay in the sea, but he chose to do so so they could be together. Sometimes, however, they left the water, especially when they got a chance to see their friends. She had yet to search for her family, but she hoped to do so one day, if she could find the courage to open up her heart again to the risk of being torn apart.

Markos opened the door for her to step in, wrapping his arms around her and pulling her into a kiss. Her heart skipped a beat as he embraced her, their kiss intensifying as their tongues entwined, the warmth of his mouth on hers sending tingles down her spine. Lifting her, he carried her to their bed chamber, laying her down on the bed and crawling over her.

"I missed you today," he said, removing her dress as if it were a delicate flower and kissing every inch of her exposed skin. The anticipation of what was to come sent her into a frenzy of desire as his hands explored her body.

"Show me." The words were like a purr, pulling a rumble from his chest.

He grinned, pushing her back onto the bed with a gentle hand. His fingers caressed her skin as he slowly undressed her, the hardness of his cock revealing his own desire. Ever since they'd settled in the palace, they couldn't seem to get their hands off each other.

Markos crawled over her, crushing his lips against hers as he wrapped her leg around his waist, sliding himself inside. As his cock filled her body, connecting them as one, a breathy moan escaped her lips. Needing more, Ocevia lifted her hips to meet his slow and steady thrusts. His hands slid to her calves, positioning her legs over his shoulders as he lifted onto his knees, the new angle shattering her completely.

Guttural moans echoed off the walls as the orgasm surged through her body, her nails tearing into the sheets trying to find purchase. Sweat dripped down his brow, his muscles flexing as he gazed down at her. Even as her body contracted and clenched, and her heart fluttered in her chest, she couldn't look away from him. She watched as his climax built, his thrusts becoming erratic as the breath whooshed out of him. The groan that rumbled out of his chest sent a shiver down her spine as his release poured into her, warming her from the inside out.

He collapsed over her as his body came down, their breaths coming in ragged gasps as their bodies trembled with the aftershocks of pleasure. When he finally rolled onto his side, he pulled her close to him, kissing her on the forehead. After everything she'd been through, happiness and contentment finally filled her, allowing her to drift off to sleep in his arms.

THE END

ENJOYED GODDESS OF DEATH?

I f you enjoyed this book, don't forget to leave a review!

Reviews are vital to authors! They help books reach new readers. I really appreciate it!

Leave a review here: https://www.amazon.com/dp/B0BHDYQ6TB

ACKNOWLEDGEMENTS

I want to thank my editor, Megan, of Willow Oak Author services for putting up with my crazy editing schedule. (At least I keep the work coming).

I would like to thank Artscandare for the font work for this book's amazing cover.

Thank you to Charlee, of Blurbs, Baubles, and Book Covers, for making my world maps.

My final thank you is to my family, friends, and most of all, my readers.

Thank you for your support!

ALSO BY C. A. VARIAN

Hazel Watson Mystery Series
Kindred Spirits: Prequel
The Sapphire Necklace
Justice for the Slain
Whispers from the Swamp
Crossroads of Death
The Spirit Collector (coming October 2023)

Crown of the Phoenix Series
Crown of the Phoenix
Crown of the Exiled
Crown of the Prophecy (Coming September 2023)

Mate of the Phoenix

Supernatural Savior Series
Song of Death
Goddess of Death
An Other World Series
The Other World
The Other Key
The Other Fate (coming January 2024)

My Alien Mate Series
My Alien Protector

Dozens of stories on Kindle Vella!

ABOUT THE AUTHOR

Raised in a small town in the heart of Louisiana's Cajun Country, C. A. Varian spent most of her childhood fishing, crabbing, and getting sunburnt at the beach. Her love of reading began very young, and she would often compete at school to read enough books to earn prizes.

Graduating with the first of her college degrees as a mother of two in her late twenties, she became a public-school teacher. As of the release of this book, she was finally able to resign from teaching to teach full time!

Writing became a passion project, and she put out her first novel in 2021, and has continued to publish new novels every few months since then, not slowing down for even a minute.

Married to a retired military officer, she spent many years moving around for his career, but they now live in central Alabama, with her youngest daughter, Arianna. Her oldest daughter, Brianna, is enjoying her happily ever after with her new husband and several pups. C. A. Varian has two Shih Tzus that she considers her children. Boy, Charlie, and girl, Luna, are their mommy's shadows. She also has three cats named Ramses, Simba, and Cookie.